HIPPOCRENE INSIDER'S GUIDE TO

POLAND

ALEXANDER JORDAN

Foreword by Jerzy Kosinski

HIPPOCRENE BOOKS
New York

For information, address
Hippocrene Books, Inc.
171 Madison Ave.
New York, NY 10016

Library of Congress Cataloging-in-Publication Data

Jordan, Alexander.
  Hippocrene insider's guide to Poland / Alexander Jordan.
  ISBN 0-87052-741-X
  1. Poland—Description and travel—1981—Guide-books.
I. Title.
DK4037.J67   1989
914.38'0456—dc19   89-1858
                                                           CIP

Printed in the United States of America.

Contents

Foreword

POLAND, by Alexander Jordan, is not an ordinary or run-of-the-mill travel guide. It is a provocative insight into Poland, the country where hospitality reigns and the American dollar wields a purchasing power many times greater than at home. It tells you how and why you can spend your next vacation, sabbatical, convalescence, or even retirement as a temporary member of the Polish community rather than as a foreign tourist.

Alex Jordan tells you how to find people in Poland who share your interests, either in your profession or in sports and hobbies, and how this can make your visit more rewarding, while at the same time reducing its costs by half or more.

The Polish tradition of hospitality deeply rooted in custom and practice, the strong pro-American orientation of the Poles, and the high value of the dollar combine to guarantee you a more cordial reception than in any other country.

Loving liberty for as long as they did and having fought for it longer than just about anybody, the Poles have been traditionally the most pro-American nation in the world. Like Americans, their keen sense of humor often has the government as its target. They have an insatiable curiosity about the outside world and that may be one reason why they will welcome you with open arms.

Now, you might ask, should you go to Poland with a view to sharing the home of someone you don't even know? Yes, why not? What if that someone is, like you, a writer, a master jeweler, an expert cook eager to share his secrets, a ballet lover, or a mountain climber? Perhaps you may learn from him (or her) as much about a different way of life as he can learn from you about the United States. Unlike some other nationalities who hold people at arm's length, the Poles are warm-hearted people with a talent for friendship. As soon as they get to know you, they will do their utmost to make your stay pleasant—and all the easier because in Poland you will become an immediate millionaire (in zlotys) even if you would have been a pauper in western Europe.

In Poland you can afford to do what perhaps you cannot afford to do at home—and do it for a few dollars per day. For instance, have you done any canoeing or boating lately? How good is your horseback riding, jumping, dressage? Are you a good fisherman, water skier, or sailor? Now, how about learning to fly a plane or a glider? Why not try hang-gliding, parachuting in free fall, or ballooning? Does your tennis, bridge, or chess need improvement? In Poland you can hire an accomplished player or coach—for as long as you wish. He or she could be a former Olympic contestant, such as you could not afford in your native America.

By staying in someone's home you are saving a fortune. The amount you pay in dollars for one day in a Warsaw hotel will pay for a month's rental of a private apartment. Your quarters could be a modern city dwelling or an old country manor, a nudist camp or a hunting lodge, a haunted castle or a rural farm.

If you feel like mixing your inner media and combining your vacation with serious study, why not give yourself a quick course in Polish art, language, or film making and do it at any one of the first-rate professional schools or universities? If your heritage is Polish, why not trace your roots—or even visit family graves? What about learning new skills? This too you can afford to do in Poland. Who knows, you may turn into a professional potter, painter, photographer, or ballet dancer.

"When I give, I give myself," said Walt Whitman. Why not give your Self the adventure of the hunt? Aside from hunting the still unspoiled lakes of the Masurian region, the Baltic coast, the spectacular Tatra mountains, wouldn't your American Self benefit from a new spiritual hunt? Learning how to share quarters with someone other than your already over-familiar Self (not to mention your by now sufficiently familiar family) is a sure way to discover the essence of the universal Self.

But, what about your Polish hosts who, though willing to share their home with you, are not at home enough in English to understand you? Will there be a language barrier between the American pro-tem guest and the pro-tem hosts? Most likely not. Thanks to their checkered history, the Poles often had occasion to learn other languages. French used to be their favorite, but it has been replaced by English, not only because Joseph Conrad Korzeniowski wrote in it, but also because it is the language of their dream land—America.

JERZY KOSINSKI

Preface

This is not a conventional guidebook of the Baedeker type, nor does it attempt detailed geographical descriptions, easily found in standard guidebooks.

Its goal is to help the visitor get to know the people of Poland by sharing with them enjoyable activities such as horseback riding, flying, kayaking, and many other sports or for those less athletically inclined, bridge, chess and cultural activities. The emphasis is not on what to see but on what to do, although the most interesting features of Poland are briefly described.

Tourists on conducted tours may see the sights but are usually isolated from the local population. POLAND assumes that one can appreciate and understand a country better by mingling with its people, and it tells you how to do it. There is no better way to make friends than by meeting those who share your interests or hobbies or by engaging together in a sport or game.

Aside from the satisfaction of getting to know the country better, the personal contacts with the local population can also result in immense savings. In every country there is a gap between the economy of the local residents and that of foreign tourists, but nowhere is it as wide as in Poland. It means that the duration of a visit could be tripled without increased cost, offering a better chance of really getting to know the country and the people. This is not possible in a week or two, and for many people cost determines the duration of their visit. The object of the advice offered in POLAND is to have more fun for less money.

Get to Know the Country Through Its People

*T*hroughout the thousand years of its history, Poland has been visited more often by invading armies than by tourists. Even now, it remains off the beaten track of international tourists, which may be a blessing for those who do venture there. Yet it is not far away. The distance between Paris and Warsaw is about half of that between New York and Miami.

An old country, Poland has a rich heritage of historic monuments, architecture and art, described in many conventional guidebooks. It can hardly compete, however, with nations such as Italy, France or England, which were never as thoroughly ravaged by invading enemies.

A perceptive foreign visitor might be interested in a different kind of society, a distinctive culture, other patterns of life and

1

thought as much as in antiquities and museums, even though they are also a part of the picture.

Many travel lovers complain that they have little contact with the people of the countries they visit, except for waiters and taxi drivers. Big hotels are pretty much the same the world over, especially if they belong to one of the major chains or to a government. They create a world of their own, no doubt comfortable but isolated from the surrounding society, bland and finally boring. Yet there are thousands of people ready to invite you to their homes as friends and do their utmost to make your visit a success. You can get to know the Polish people as well as the country although there is no universal method of doing so.

While the governments of most of Poland's neighbors discourage contacts between their citizens and foreigners, sometimes prohibiting them, there are no such restrictions in Poland and no rules against fraternization with foreign visitors, providing that no political activities are involved.

Neither are there any such rules in France, yet getting to know the French people on a personal level is notoriously difficult. They tolerate tourists, as long as they bring in profit, but carefully avoid any personal involvement. Foreigners have been known to live in France for years before they were invited to a French family home.

In total contrast, Polish people are always ready and eager to welcome foreign guests—perhaps because they have seldom been numerous. They also feel that meeting people of various nationalities is the next best thing to traveling abroad, which is difficult for them because of their currency restrictions. They are as interested in you as you may be in them.

In most countries of western Europe, small hotels and inns provide a meeting ground with the natives on terms less formal than the Hiltons and Intercontinentals but still far short of a personal social interaction. Such small hotels and guest

2

houses are scarce in Poland, as are mom and pop restaurants, charming bistros, and pubs.

On the other hand, the tradition of hospitality and the interest in foreign guests are incomparably stronger in Poland. How to establish first contact will be our main concern.

The language barrier may appear at first as a major obstacle, but it is far less serious than you might think. Unlike Americans, the Poles eagerly learn foreign languages, first and foremost among them English. In the major cities and towns, which is where you are most likely to be, roughly one person in six or seven will have some knowledge of English. Among young people the percentage might be higher. Those unfamiliar with English usually find quickly a friend who is and who can serve as interpreter.

Long waiting lines outside stores are a common sight in Poland, but I was amazed in Warsaw when I saw one several blocks long, with hundreds of men and women waiting patiently for hours in rather cool weather. I considered joining the line, thinking they must have been waiting for something highly desirable, the bargain of the century, perhaps. I asked what it could be and the answer was: "We are waiting to enroll in the English classes offered by American Baptist missionaries."

A large portion of Poles have relatives in the United States, some of who visit Poland from time or time or invite their kinsmen to America as guests. The line outside the U.S. consulate in Warsaw is almost as long as the one for English lessons. Consequently, many people have a fair knowledge of American life; though few Americans know anything about Poland. Actually Poland differs in this respect from other East European countries, which also have have many emigrants in America, but in smaller numbers. There are more Polish Americans than Czechoslovakian, Hungarian, Bulgarian, Rumanian, and Lithuanian together. The number of Ameri-

3

cans of Polish descent is estimated at about 8 million, making them one of the largest ethnic groups in the United States, though certainly not the most vocal or assertive.

A nation with a thousand years of history, Poland has an abundance of historic monuments, art treasures and other relics. Most tour guides concentrate on them—and rightly so—but that is precisely the reason why no attempt will be made to describe them here. This omission should not be interpreted as neglect, quite the contrary. It recognizes that the number of places worth seeing in Poland is so vast that it requires a separate volume. Many such books exist, for example *Introduction to Poland* by Budrewicz (American Institute of Polish Culture, 1440 79th Street Causeway, Miami, FL 33141), which offers a light and amusing general view of Poland's attractions. Other books offer detailed descriptions of Poland's antiquities and sights.

The objective here is not what to see in Poland, but what to do, with emphasis on activities that may bring the visitor in closer contact with the Polish people. The best way to meet people is to find common interests and engage together in an activity enjoyed by both parties. The people of Poland are at least as worth knowing as its ancient castles, monasteries and churches. They are themselves an ancient nation, the direct descendants of the country's inhabitants of several thousand years ago. That is not the case of many other European nations, formed by the great migrations of the early Middle Ages. Poland is one of the most homogenous nations of Europe, more so than Great Britain with its Scots, Welshmen, and Irishmen in Ulster; or France with the sharp contrast between north and south that is also true of Italy.

Actually the people of Poland are a tribe as much as a nation, resembling in that respect the Japanese. They are like one large family of about 38 million people, heading fast to the 40 million mark. The move of several million Poles from the east to the west after World War II helped to mingle them

4

into one group, with most regional characteristics dispersed in the mix. They are also united by their language, with its rich literature, and their religion (95% Catholic).

That tribal cohesion may be the reason why the Poles remain steadfast in their desire for independence and resist any attempts of foreign influence.

Aside from the natural desire to get to know the people of the country we visit, there are also practical advantages in knowing them. Few commercial advertisements appear in the Polish press and even these would mean little to you. Neither are there any Yellow Pages in the telephone directory, which is very hard to get anyway. As a result it is not easy to find anything you might be looking for, such as shops, restaurants, rooms, or entertainments. Local residents, however, have a very efficient grapevine system by which they learn what is to be found where and when. It is difficult to get anything done in Poland without having access to that system, that is, to some friendly people. Having such friends can cut a foreign visitor's expenses by half or more and make all the difference between enjoying a good time and groping in the dark.

What to Take to Poland, What Not to Take

*T*ake no food or liquor—both can be easily purchased in Poland, especially Scotch whiskies and cognac, at less than half the stateside prices. Moreover, they are the same well-known brands, such as Johnny Walker and others. One can even get genuine Havana cigars for a fraction of their cost in western Europe (they are banned in the U.S.A.) There is no need to bring cosmetics, unless one is fussy about a particular brand. Most popular American brands can be purchased for dollars in the Pewex stores, also for less than at home. There is also no point in bringing gift items such as tea or coffee, which are available in the Pewex stores.

However, if you happen to need regular medications, especially prescription ones, be sure to take an adequate supply. If you plan to have some dental work done, it would also be a good idea to bring some of the materials required, such as the various amalgams and cements. Even if not used by you, they would serve as effective barter for whatever might be needed. The savings on dental work performed in Poland can be staggering—a fraction of the American price. The dental materials, however, are in short supply and would be greatly appreciated. Some very ordinary items, for example tape, white correcting fluid, good typing paper and other stationery are hard to get.

Be sure that your cameras or other electronic gadgets have fresh batteries, as new ones may be unobtainable. Electric watch batteries, on the other hand, are abundant and cheaper than at home. Spectacles can be readily replaced at a fraction of the original cost and just as good.

Ready-made clothes and shoes are not very stylish in Poland, but you can order custom-made footwear and garments, which will be much less expensive than anything made to measure in the West. There are many excellent shoemakers, tailors and dressmakers to be found, as so many other things, mainly by word of mouth recommendation. As a general rule, anything hand made is a bargain, while high-technology items are not available or expensive. It might be desirable to bring a length of worsted, tweed or other fabric for your tailor or dressmaker as the local choice is limited. The principle of saving on labor costs and supplying the raw materials can also be applied to jewelry. If you wish to have a piece of old jewelry restyled, or made into something else, the cost in Poland will be much lower than elsewhere. However, declare the item to the Polish customs bureau on entry, so that there will be no trouble taking it out of the country. That would apply only if a major piece is involved; smaller ones are seldom noticed.

Polish experts in the renovation of art works are among the best in the world and the savings on even a single job could pay for a trip of several weeks.

As far as presents are concerned, it might be a good idea to bring some of the small solar-powered calculators, which sell in America for $5 or less and are rather scarce in Poland. Clothes would also be appreciated, bearing in mind that warm woolens are more useful in the north than flimsy summer dresses.

Visas and Travel Regulations

*A*ll persons intending to visit Poland must obtain a visa at a Polish embassy or consulate. Applications should be made at least ten days before departure. You need a valid passport, two photographs and a fee of $15. In some cases visas have been obtained within 24 hours, but one should not count on it.

Visitors are required to effect a change of currency to Polish zlotys, at the official exchange rate, which is about 450 zlotys to the dollar (the amounts vary). The amount to be changed is $15 per day. Payment may be made either at authorized travel offices in the country of origin (notably at branches of the Polish Orbis travel office) or at the border. Persons making the payment abroad receive vouchers that are one-way exchangeable for Polish currency or that can be used for payment in Poland. The change offices at the border give zlotys in cash.

If you wish to extend your stay, permission can be obtained at the local militia office, which will require the exchange of hard currency for zlotys in the same daily amount of $15.

The mandatory currency exchange does not apply to persons under 16 years of age, and reduced rates of mandatory exchange are available for the following:

Persons of Polish origin, their spouses and children, are required to change only $7 per day

The same reduced rate applies to the spouses of students enrolled in studies in Poland and also to the following:

Persons under age 21

Students over age 21 if they are members of the International Student Union (with a valid membership card) or the International Student Travel Conference

Persons intending to camp in Poland between May 1 and September 30, if they cross the border in a car with a trailer or a caravan

Persons arriving in Poland by yacht or renting a yacht in Poland

A special rate of $3 exchange per day applies to persons of Polish descent after the 31st day of their sojourn in Poland

Persons in transit, spending up to 72 hours in Poland, are required to make the appropriate exchange only for one day. Double check these regulations when you apply. They do change.

The "Polish descent" clause seems to be interpreted flexibly (except in hotels). A Polish surname, knowledge of the language or other evidence of Polish origin would probably be enough.

Persons legally earning zlotys in Poland, for example, performers, English teachers or other professionals, may be released from the mandatory currency exchange. This would apply only to moneys earned from official institutions, not from private individuals or companies. Zlotys earned in this manner can be deposited in a Polish bank and their value is that they can be used, for example, to purchase tickets from the Polish airline LOT. Otherwise, non-Polish citizens have to pay for them in hard currency, at a far higher cost. LOT flies, among other places, to Bangkok in Thailand. The fare in zlotys is a fraction of that charged in dollars.

The reason for the regulation requiring foreigners to change a certain sum per day through official channels in this: the unofficial rate of exchange is at least four times the official one. Consequently, if no one changed hard currency at the official rate, the Polish treasury would suffer. Without the mandatory daily quota, everyone would get about 3,000 zlotys for the dollar rather than 450.

How to Get to Poland: The LOT Airlines

Contrary to what one might think, LOT is not an acronym—it simply means flight in Polish.

The national Polish airline, founded in 1929, has operated ever since, interrupted only from 1939 to 1945, when the Polish pilots were employed flying Spitfires in the Battle of Britain rather than guiding civilian airliners.

LOT flies nonstop from New York to Warsaw, leaving JFK airport in New York at 4 p.m. and arriving in Warsaw, at 6:20 a.m. the following day. It also flies from O'Hare airport in Chicago, departing at 9:30 p.m. and arriving in Warsaw at 3:20 p.m. the following day.

In addition to its scheduled flights, LOT also offers various charter and guided-tour package deals. Information about them can be obtained at LOT offices as follows:

How to Get to Poland: The LOT Airlines

In New York at 500 Fifth Avenue, phone (212) 869-1074, or toll free from out of state 800-223-0593.

In Chicago at 333 North Michigan Avenue, Suite 1016, phone (312) 658-5656.

In Los Angeles at 6420 Wilshire Boulevard, Suite 410, phone (213) 658-5656.

Reservations and bookings can also be made, of course, at any travel agency.

Readers of our guide will have noticed its emphasis on meeting people and making friends as the key to knowing Poland. This is where flying LOT offers certain advantages. Most passengers on LOT flights to Poland are either Polish Americans or Poles returning to their country. A long flight provides plenty of opportunities for getting to know some of them and receiving many useful hints on arranging a pleasant and inexpensive stay in Poland. Most passengers on the Warsaw flight have some knowledge of English and will be eager to help non-Polish visitors find their way in Poland. Making Polish friends can start even before setting foot in the country and it can go a long way in making the first days easier and less expensive.

LOT also flies to all the major cities of Europe and has offices in them, so that if you find yourself in Paris, London, Frankfurt or any other western Europe city, getting to Poland is easy.

Yet perhaps the LOT network outside of Europe is the most interesting part of its services. It flies regularly to Cairo in Egypt, Istanbul in Turkey, Larnaca on Cyprus, Damascus in Syria, Baghdad in Iraq, Abu Dhabi-Dubai in the Gulf, Delhi in India, Bangkok in Thailand, and Beijing (Peking) in China.

The "Week in Bangkok" tours are very popular in Poland and not only because of the joys promised by the legendary pleasures of the most wide-open city in the East, perhaps in the world. Though not insensitive to the charms of Thai culture, Polish tourists have other objectives. They leave Warsaw loaded with various goods known to be in demand in Thailand. They sell them in Bangkok and with the proceeds, buy items which are cheap there but costly in Europe. This display of entrepreneurial skill permits the knowledgeable tourist to make the trip to the exotic sin dens of the East at no cost, and sometimes with a small profit. The same procedure is also practiced on other runs outside Europe, but Bangkok is surely more fun than Kuwait and enjoys a unique reputation for voluptuous ambiance.

The commercial operation is quite legal, as the tourists pay customs duties where required, and even after deducting surplus luggage weight charges, they end up in the black.

We cannot advise you what merchandise to take, as we have never made the trip and the demand varies frequently. It should not be difficult, however, to find people in Warsaw who might share their know-how with American friends. Aside from any commercial ventures, a visit to the Far East via Poland could cost much less than by other routes. The principle mentioned earlier applies here also: the Polish passengers on a Bangkok flight would be the ones to tell you how to enjoy a visit there without paying Hilton or Intercontinental hotel rates. Living with a very weak currency (the Polish zloty) the Poles have had to develop the art of having a good time at little cost. Coupled with just a few dollars, this art could translate into a super good time.

Flying via Warsaw could also enhance savings for those headed for other Eastern countries, as well as Australia, as there are numerous connections at Bangkok.

LOT also flies to all the neighboring "socialist" countries. The central location of Warsaw makes it a good starting point for visiting Hungary, Bulgaria, Rumania, or even the Soviet Union.

The LOT domestic flights between Polish cities are perhaps

of lesser interest, as the distances are too slight to justify flying, especially when fast rail connections such as the nonstop Warsaw to Cracow express are available. The 200-mile trip takes just three hours, which is comparable to the New York to Washington Metroliners.

Customs Regulations

Visitors may bring in, in addition to personal belongings and items of daily use, gifts not in excess in 10,000 zlotys in value, one liter of wine and one liter of spirits, 250 cigarettes or 50 cigars or 250 grams of tobacco. Persons under age 17 are not allowed the exemption of liquors and tobacco.

Items such as cameras, radios, tape recorders, sports equipment, canoes less than 5.5 meters long, two sporting guns with 100 cartridges for each, handguns and 25 cartridges, jewelry and furs may be brought in, provided that they are taken out of the country on departure. They must be declared on arrival at the border or airport and presented again on departure.

Cars are admitted for one year, after which they must leave the country. Cars of foreign registration, if sold in Poland, are subject to heavy import duties, which make such sales difficult or impractical.

Prohibited items include illegal drugs, weapons and explosives, printing and duplication equipment, pornography, maps with German names of Polish cities, and literature considered harmful to the interest of the People's Republic of Poland.

When leaving the country, visitors may take out free of duty: all the items declared at their entry; 250 cigarettes, 50 cigars or 250 grams of tobacco; 5 liters of alcoholic beverages (not allowed for those under age 17); goods purchased for hard currency in authorized stores (such as Pewex or Baltona) with appropriate bills; works of art, paintings and others, regardless of their value, executed by artists living after May 9, 1945, and purchased in the government Desa or Cepelia stores (with bills of sale proof). The exportation of antiques is prohibited, except by written authorization of the Conservator of Art Works.

Other items may be subject to export duties. The authorities are particularly concerned with the exportation of art treasures, as there have been cases—especially in the years immediately following the war—of priceless art works illegally smuggled out of the country. Such practices are particularly resented in a country that suffered cruel losses from wartime looting.

Currency Regulations

*V*isitors may bring with them any amount of foreign currency in cash, traveler's checks, or other financial instruments. Such funds must be declared on entry and the amounts noted on a card retained by the bearer.

Visitors are not permitted to take out of the country on their departure more funds or traveler's checks than they brought in.

The bringing in or taking out of Polish currency is prohibited.

All the major credit cards—American Express, Diners Club, Eurocard, MasterCard, Visa and others—are honored by the Polish official agencies, such as the Orbis travel offices and hotels, though not by retail stores. Keep in mind that some official agencies set limits on credit card use.

Foreign currency can be exchanged for zlotys in principle only through banks or authorized exchange offices, at the official rate, which is (at the time of writing) about 600 zlotys to the U.S. dollar.

The black market rate, which might be called "gray market," is published daily in the press. It is currently over 3,000 zlotys to the dollar, that is, approximately four times the official rate. The gray aspect of the situation lies in the fact that vouchers in dollar denominations, sold by Polish offices abroad and called *bony*, can be sold legally to anyone. The line between selling actual dollar bills and the bony in the same denominations is a thin one.

Unlike other "socialist" countries, Poland allows its citizens to possess foreign currency, which in practice means U.S. dollars. Polish citizens may also open dollar accounts, bearing interest at 9%, in state banks. The amount of U.S. dollars in circulation in Poland is estimated by news reports to be several billions. That is why the Pewex stores, in which the price tags are in dollars, do a roaring business. There are about 600 such stores in Poland, maybe a dozen in Warsaw alone. People shopping there are not asked where they got their dollars—they are mostly gifts from relatives abroad or money earned by taking a temporary job in a foreign country.

The practical fact is that the dollar is in general circulation in Poland and is eagerly accepted in payment.

Remember, however, foreign visitors must change officially $15 (or its equivalent in other currencies) for each day of their residence in Poland, or half that amount if they are students or persons of Polish origin.

Beware of street money changers who will accost you. Many are shady characters capable of cheating you.

Communications: Post Office and Telephones

*L*etter delivery between Poland and foreign countries takes a long time, so don't be surprised if your postcards arrive home after you do. The post office, however, can render you a useful service by taking care of surplus luggage that you do not want to drag around anymore. It can be sent home by parcel post.

The main post offices have a stand where whatever you wish to send is packed very professionally into a sturdy parcel. Not part of the post office service, this service is a concession operated for public convenience. It supplies carton boxes, wrapping paper, plastic foam balls for delicate items, strong string and everything required for a solid parcel. I saw even crystal wine glasses packed so they would not break—I hope. The charge is nominal and the service a great convenience.

The telephone service is often erratic. The trick is to dial slowly. If you dial too fast, the equipment does not seem to keep pace with you and you get odd noises instead of the ringing sound. Try again slowly and you will eventually get your number.

Direct dialing service is available to most European countries, but not overseas. It is also available between the major Polish cities, but not to small towns.

If you want to call the United States, for example, you must first call the international exchange (dial 901) and ask for connection with the overseas number required (the international operator would have some knowledge of English). Then wait until they get the number for you. If the lines are busy, it could take hours.

It is possible, however, to dial directly from the United States to Poland. Consequently, if you want to keep in touch with home it would be best to arrange with your family and friends to call you at hours when you can be waiting for a call. This is far simpler than trying to reach an American number from Poland.

This is another example of friends being almost a necessity. They can provide you with a permanent base and a number to be called, whereas if you are moving all over the country, your family would have no way of reaching you fast. A hotel or office could not render this service, because of their changing personnel and the fact that many calls are made at hours when hotel staff is unavailable.

Directional codes for direct dialing to some European cities

Amsterdam—0-03120
Belgrade   —8038-11

Budapest   —0-0361
London   —0-0441
Madrid   —0034-1
Moscow   —0-07095
Paris   —8033-1
Prague   —0-042-2
Rome   —8039-6
Stockholm —8046-8
Vienna   —0-043222
West Berlin —0-0372
Zurich   —0-041-1

For domestic intercity calls, dial 900; for foreign calls dial 901. Some other useful telephone numbers include (in Warsaw):

Police (called *Milicja*)—997
Fire department—998
Medical emergency—999

Personal Safety

*M*ost guidebooks discreetly pass over the problem of personal safety. Yet some foreign visitors to Miami—and a few other places—might be alive today had they been forewarned.

I use Miami as an example because it happens to be my home. The yearly number of murders in Miami (population 1.5 million) is greater than in Poland with its 38 million people. Actually about 500 homicides occur a year in Poland, and slightly more in Dade County. This means, in practical terms, that you need have little fear walking at night the streets of Warsaw or any other Polish city.

The low rate of violent crime in Poland is due to many factors: a homogenous population with a strong family structure, the powerful moral influence of the Catholic church, the total absence of handguns in private hands, a relatively insignificant level of drug addiction, and, last but not least, stern judges concerned more with public safety than with the alleged rights and privileges of criminals. Murders do occur occasionally, but a vicious killer could not escape justice by playing an endless game of motions and appeals.

This is not to say that the Poles are a bunch of choirboys.

POLAND

Ordinary larceny is not uncommon, so watch your purse and pocket as you would in any other country and steer clear of characters offering to change dollars in the street at an ostensibly favorable rate. They might hand you a wad of zlotys with 1,000 bill denominations on top and lower ones inside. Incidentally, although changing currency outside of banks is forbidden, this law is not enforced as rigidly as in Russia or other socialist countries.

The dollar vouchers, which can be used in payment at the Pewex stores, can be sold legally to anyone. It is also quite legal for Polish citizens to have foreign currency in their possession, or else they could not shop in any of the 600 Pewex stores scattered throughout the country.

The main fact is that your life and limb are not in danger and muggings are rare. Oddly enough, a foreigner is even less at risk than a native because the hoodlums realize that they will be punished more severely for robbing a guest.

Quarters

A roof over one's head is the first thing a traveler must think about and often the major item in his budget. Unlike western European countries, Poland does not have a multitude of small hotels and inns. The hotels in major cities are government controlled—and we all know what that means. In Warsaw there are several allegedly first-class hotels: Victoria, Forum, the Europejski, and Solec. Foreign guests are compelled to pay in hard currency and the prices are about the same as those in London or New York.

There are also more modest hotels, but their rates are not cheap either, relative to the comforts they offer. Owing to the shortage of hotel rooms, most cities have bureaus that handle the rental of rooms in private homes. They are called Biuro Kwaterunkowe, or quartering office.

The rooms are usually quite satisfactory, as they must meet certain standards to be listed. The price is, of course, much lower. Rooming in private homes brings the visitor in closer touch with the local residents. Polish people are very hospitable and generally treat visitors not as customers but as personal guests. They volunteer all kinds of help without necessarily expecting special remuneration although a small gift might be appreciated.

Such assistance is necessary in a country where there is little advertising (and all of it in Polish), no Yellow Pages and no way to find shops, restaurants or various services unless guided by a native.

Another reason for the eagerness of people to serve as guides is the fact that they, or their children, are probably anxious to practice their English. In most households in major cities—and many smaller ones too—someone is trying to learn English, so an English-speaking visitor is doubly welcome.

In case one plans to stay a week or more, it is often possible to rent a small apartment, fully equipped, with telephone and all facilities. This is, of course, only possible through people one has met on a personal basis, but such acquaintances are sometimes formed quickly.

The weekly cost of such a rental is usually less than the price of a hotel room for one day. In many cases, single persons are willing to rent their apartments while they move in with their relatives for a week or two.

The housing situation in Poland is completely different from that in the United States. Apartments are extremely hard to get, but once acquired they cost little. Unlike the American, who sometimes spends as much as a third of his income on housing, the Pole spends perhaps 10% of his salary on housing, but much more on food. Consequently renting an apartment to a foreigner for $25 a week makes a lot of sense.

When renting rooms with a family, meals may be included and Polish home cooking is generally far better than restaurant fare. Aside from the savings, the greatest benefit of such arrangements is getting to know the country much better than can be done by people who only meet waiters and taxi drivers.

While adequate, such accommodations are generally not up to American standards. The bathrooms are often old-fashioned, the corridors narrow, and the staircases messy. If

26

you are looking for a Howard Johnson's, this is not your cup of tea, but for budget-minded people, eager to see how the local residents live, it is an interesting experience.

The suggested method of finding such quarters is to stop at some minor hotel or a student dormitory in the summer—of which more later—and contact organizations concerned with your particular area of interest. Within a few days you will know people willing to help you to find whatever you may be looking for.

During summer vacations, the dormitories of many universities and colleges function as student hostels. Although theoretically intended for student tourists, they are actually also available for foreign visitors of any age. A single room might cost about $4 a day and a double $6. Not all the rooms have individual bathrooms.

Tourist information offices (identified by the initials I.T.) will help find such facilities.

Bureaus for Renting Rooms in Private Homes

State-controlled offices have lists of private homes in which rooms may be rented. The rooms must conform to certain standards, which means that while by no means luxurious, they will be reasonably clean. The prices range between 2,000 and 3,000 zlotys a day, payable in zlotys purchased and confirmed by a receipt at the official rate. That condition is not always enforced in private transactions. The following offices listed by city, street address, and phone can help you find lodging in private homes:

Cracow: Pawia 8, phone 22-19-21
Gdansk: Elzbietanska 10, phone 31-26-34

Lodz: Plac Wolnosci 10/11, phone 687-45
Lublin: Narutowicza 19, phone 296-85
Olsztyn: Aleja Wojska Polskiego 14, phone 660-41
Poznan: Glogowska 16, phone 603-13
Rzeszow: Aleja 22 Lipca 2, phone 374-41
Szczecin: Jednosci Narodowej 50, phone 464-31
Warsaw: Krucza 17, phone 28-75-40
Wroclaw: Swierczewskiego 98, phone 44-41-01
Zakopane: Kosciuszki 236, phone 21-51

In addition to the above offices, there are others in smaller towns. Very often, landladies stroll in front of the office and try to get customers before the customers consult the I.T. office.

Transportation

*P*assenger traffic is carried mainly by the railroads, which provide good service throughout the country. Several main lines have electric traction; others use diesel locomotives and rumor has it that steam engines may be seen on some local runs in rural areas.

The Warsaw–Cracow express takes only three hours to travel 200 miles nonstop. Its average speed of 70 miles per hour compares favorably with most Amtrak trains. The trains usually run on time.

The fares are very reasonable, but the trains are often packed and it is advisable to buy reservation tickets, which entitle you to a numbered seat on the train. It is better to go first class, which costs a little more but is worth it. On the longer night runs, there are sleeping cars which also have to be reserved through a travel office or at the station.

Domestic air connections are available, but the distances are not great enough to justify the trouble of getting to the airport and from the airport on arrival. Besides, air fares have to be paid by foreigners in dollars, whereas rail tickets can be purchased by anyone for zlotys.

POLAND

Smaller towns and rural districts are served by buses. There
are bus terminals in practically all the towns and many villages. The buses provide a good service, but are often
crowded. The fares are nominal.

Taxi fares are moderate and it sometimes pays to use a taxi
to get to a destination fifty miles away or more. Taxi drivers do
not object, especially if it is a round trip and a good tip is
thrown in or a price negotiated in advance—preferably in
dollars.

The government-run Orbis travel office offers car rentals,
with driver or without, at prices several times higher than in
the United States and payable only in hard currency. It may be
possible, however, to arrange a car loan privately on much
more favorable terms. As so many other things, this requires
personal contacts, and that is why ways of making them are
emphasized.

If a car is brought from abroad, gasoline vouchers must be
purchased for hard currency at a price much bigger than the
cost of gasoline at the pump for Polish citizens, whose
monthly gasoline consumption is rationed. However, the cost
of the gasoline vouchers for foreigners is no higher than in
western Europe, though about triple the U.S. price. Gasoline
is also sold at some stations described as *Komercjalna* at 1,200
zlotys a gallon, or about the U.S. price. The rationing does
not apply to diesel fuel, which can be purchased freely at a low
price. Consequently, if you want to visit Poland by car, a diesel
engine car is most desirable. Diesel cars are in great demand in
Poland, but selling them is not easy because of the very high
customs duties.

Traffic is fairly heavy in the major cities and the visitor is
surprised to see that parking on the sidewalks is permitted; one
just drives over the curb and parks diagonally.

International driving permits, which can be obtained in the
United States from the AAA, American Automobile Association, are recognized in Poland.

When bringing a foreign car into Poland, one should make sure that it is in good condition and not likely to require repairs. Polish mechanics are skilled and resourceful, but parts for foreign cars are hard to get. The only makes for which parts might be obtainable are Fiat, Volkswagen and Peugeot—and even then one has to be lucky to find the right part in stock.

Practically all the cars on Polish roads are Fiats manufactured locally on license. The most popular model is the tiny subcompact Fiat 126, currently called *Maluch* ("kid"). It is nominally a four seater, but the passengers in the back seat should be preferably children or midgets. Nevertheless, it is a handy little car in city traffic and is very thrifty on gas. It can be purchased for $2,500—surely the world's greatest car bargain.

There are also the Fiat 125, a 1,500-cc, regular four-door compact—which costs about $3,500, and the upscale *Polonez* elegantly styled at about $4,250.

All these cars can be ordered through the Orbis travel offices abroad for delivery on arrival in Poland.

Buying one for use in Poland and then reselling it in France or Italy (where these models are known) might be the cheapest way of enjoying the use of a car in Poland, though this method would of course only be sensible for a fairly prolonged visit. It is also possible to give such a car as a gift to a relative or friend in Poland.

On the whole, the Polish roads are good and the traffic outside of towns very light because of the gas rationing. The highways are well marked and there are excellent road maps so that touring is quite easy. Gas stations and service garages, however, are relatively few and sometimes difficult to find.

Car Rental

The wide gap in price between the conventional, official tourist arrangements and those made through private contacts is nowhere more evident than in the rental of automobiles.

The big companies, such as Hertz or Avis, in cooperation with the state Orbis travel office, offer weekly rentals of such automobiles as the Polonez, which is the upscale model of the Polish Fiat, a four-door sedan with a 1,500-cc engine.

If one contemplates a stay of several weeks, the same model or an equivalent can be rented privately for about $25 a week or the corresponding amount in zlotys, a fraction of the Hertz or Avis fee. It is true that this requires some effort and may be impractical for short periods. Knowledge of Polish is also necessary, but that is not a serious obstacle, as it is always possible to find an English-speaking local resident willing to help. As in many other situations, such assistance is invaluable and that is why we never tire of suggesting ways of finding Polish friends.

The procedure is simple. Place a classified ad in the *Zycie Warszawy* daily when in Warsaw, or in the leading local

newspaper in any other city. "Wanted, car for hire for ____
weeks." You might want to specify that it should be a standard-
size car rather than the "mini-mini" Fiat 126, which accounts
for most of the Polish cars because of its fuel economy and low
price. It is reliable for city driving and easy to park, but it's also
a rather tight fit for anyone over 5'6" and not the perfect
vehicle for a long trip.

Such an advertisement will bring many replies. Of course
you'll need to have a telephone number to which they can be
addressed. Then it is only a matter of choosing the best car and
the most favorable terms. The reason this method works in
Poland but not in other countries is that, because of the gas
rationing, many people can use their cars only part of the
time. Rather than have them standing idle, they may be
willing to rent to a reliable person for a couple of weeks.

The foreign guest must have an international driving license, issued by the AAA (American Automobile Association). He will not be short of fuel, which he can buy at the gas
stations selling *komercyalna*, that is, gasoline at a higher price,
but without ration cards. The price of about 1,200 zlotys a
gallon is prohibitive for many Polish drivers, but is rather less
than the U.S. price and only a fraction of the price charged in
western Europe.

Automobile insurance in Poland covers authorized drivers
other than the owner and additional insurance can be obtained at little cost. The procedure described here is, of
course, only worth undertaking when a longer stay is con-
templated. For shorter visits the taxis provide convenient transportation at minimal cost. The only problem is that they are
not supposed to be hailed in the street, but only at designated
spots, where usually a waiting line has formed. You can,
however, order taxis by telephone.

The peculiar feature of Polish taxis is that they are available
for trips of any distance. A taxi driver is usually willing to take

a passenger even a hundred miles away, if it is a round trip. The price may be according to the meter or negotiated in advance, but it is moderate. That is why, when driving in the country, one is sometimes surprised by the sight of a city taxi.

Hitchhiking

Hitchhiking is officially recognized in Poland as a legitimate means of transportation.

Between May and the end of September, persons wishing to hitchhike may purchase, for the modest sum of 300 zlotys, a book of vouchers good for a certain travel distance, in kilometers of course. Good for 2,000 kilometers, the voucher book can be purchased in tourist offices at the highway entry points, the I.T. information stations, and some other travel offices. The drivers who offer transportation later receive compensation for the vouchers collected; there are even prizes for those having the most vouchers.

When driving along Poland's highways, you will be asked often for a ride—with no vouchers involved. Because of the official endorsement of the practice, the persons asking for a lift are not vagabonds or shady individuals; they are usually perfectly respectable people, young and old, who will try to compensate you with a few bills as they leave.

Actually taking on people who wave you for a ride may sometimes be an interesting experience if they happen to speak

35

a language you know such as English, French or German, which is often the case.

There is little risk in taking on a hitchhiker in Poland though one must exercise some judgment in sizing up the person. The chance of coming to any harm is minimal. There is no embarrassment in asking for a ride, as there would be in some countries. Few people own cars in rural districts and the bus service may not always be available at the time, so asking a passing driver for a lift is a perfectly sensible solution to the transportation problem and requires no apology. The riders are generally polite; they will not light a cigarette without asking permission and they behave correctly.

The guest in your car may turn out to be a blessing, as he or she will help you to find the right route, advise you on available accommodations or facilities, or even invite you home.

As to active hitchhiking; that is, asking for rides, it is an option open to those who like the idea. Their chances of getting a ride are slight because the traffic on highways is light and one might have to wait very long for a passing car.

Cycling

*C*ycling is surely the cheapest mode of transportation and the one that brings the traveler into closest contact with the country and the people. (Of course, walking, like the pilgrims on their way to the Czestochowa shrine, rates even better on these counts, except that lay tourists may not seek mortification of the flesh as a worthy goal.)

Student tourists from neighboring countries, such as Hungary, often visit Poland on bicycles, usually in packs of a dozen or so boys and girls.

Some countries do not lend themselves to this type of travel, for example those with bad roads, good roads with heavy traffic, steep hills, danger of robbery, or worse. None of these conditions apply to Poland. The roads are good and lightly traveled. Most of the terrain is fairly flat (except for the Carpathian region), and personal safety is better than in many more developed countries, not to mention those less developed.

In the 1930s a British writer and friend, Bernard Newman, made it a habit to visit a country by bicycle and then write a book about it. The books were called *Pedalling France, Pedall-*

37

ing Poland, and so on. He even wrote *Pedalling Russia.* This was no mean feat at a time when millions were starving in Stalin's Gulag, and an Englishman on a bicycle might easily be taken for a madman or a spy or both.

It was possible for a foreigner to tour Poland on a bicycle fifty years ago in perfect safety and it is also safe to do so today. Naturally, Newman toured in the summer, as riding a bicycle through several feet of snow might be foolhardy. Summer weather also gave him the option of sleeping in a haystack if lodging was not found. Most of the time he probably slept in a farmer's house, and so could any presentday tourist for the deeper one goes into the country, the more hospitable the people.

One thing is sure, Bernard Newman knew a whole lot more about the countries he visited than do conventional tourists who stay in the smart hotels. Of course this style of traveling is not to everyone's liking and it helps to be young to enjoy it to the full, though there are always exceptions. One sure way for that kind of tourist to get help and hospitality everywhere would be to fly a small flag with American colors on his handlebars. Poles have very friendly feelings toward the United States and welcome Americans with open arms.

Camping

*P*oland has about 240 camping grounds, with 54,000 places. They are divided into three classes: First-class grounds, of which there are about 60, have cold and hot running water through the day, flushing toilet facilities, tourist kitchens, cafeteria service, and facilities for hooking up a caravan to a 220-volt power supply. Second-class camps have similar facilities on a smaller scale and hot water only in the morning and evening. There are about 100 of them. Third-class camps, of which there are about 80, offer more Spartan facilities. Some of the camps have cabins for rent. The camping grounds are located near major cities and in popular tourist areas.

Fees for camp use are moderate. It is most advisable to make reservations, especially for camps along the seacoast and in the mountain regions, by writing or calling the camps selected.

Information on the location of the camping sites is available in the international camping guidebooks published in Europe; at the Orbis travel offices, and at the headquarters of the Polish Camping Federation, Krolewska 27, Warsaw, phone 26-80-89; and at all I.T. (Tourist Information) stations throughout Poland.

Maps showing the location of all the camps can be obtained at the Ruch newsstands throughout the country.

Youth Hostels

*T*here are in Poland about 1,500 youth hostels. Controlled by the Polish Federation of Youth Hostels, which is affiliated with the International Youth Hostel Federation, most of them are in school buildings and consequently are available only during the summer vacation period. A list of the 200 best ones can be found in the International Youth Hostel handbook. It is advisable to make a reservation by writing to the hostels on your itinerary.

Any person over 10 years of age can use the hostels. There is no upper age limit.

The prices are low, with a further 25% discount for members of the International Youth Hostel Federation. Membership cards can be obtained in Warsaw, at Chocimska 28, phone 49-83-54, for a fee of $10 for adults and $5 for youths under age 21. A visitor can stay no more than three or four days in the same hostel.

International Student Hotels

The travel office Almatur manages low-priced hotels located during the summer vacation (July–September) in college dormitories. They are open to the general public, but card-carrying members of the I.S.T.C., a student travel association, are entitled to discounts from the already very low prices, ranging from about $4 to $6 daily. There are single, double, and three-person rooms.

The standard of comfort and service is, of course, not equal to that of commercial hotels, but not at all bad for the price.

The principal international student hotels, listed by city, are the following:

Cracow: 29 Listopada 48a, phone 11-80-60
Czestochowa: Dekabrystow 26/30, phone 573-75
Gdansk: Wyspianskiego 5a, phone 41-00-88
Katowice: Medykow 18, phone 52-38-60
Lublin: Nadbystrzycka 2, phone 55-71-33
Poznan: Obornicka 84b, phone 23-24-97
Szczecin: Dunikowskiego 4, phone 82-29-31
Warsaw: Warynskiego 12, phone 25-52-01; also Nowoursynowska 161
Wroclaw: Olszewskiego 235, phone 48-64-76

There are also such hotels in Bialystok, Bydgoszcz, Gliwice, Kielce, Koszalin, Lodz, Olsztyn, Opole, Rzeszow, Torun, and Zielona Gora.

Shopping

Poland can hardly claim to be a shopper's paradise; it's more of a purgatory. Most goods abundant in the West are in short supply and often of poor quality. This is true of mass-produced items sold in department stores, but it is quite a different story when we talk about artisans' handmade work.

In the side streets of Warsaw, sometimes in backyards or basements, one can find many small boutiques selling all kinds of hand-crafted articles, some of them exquisite or made to order. They cost far less than comparable custom made goods in the West.

These small shops, privately owned, are not easy to find, though some streets, for example, Rutkowskiego, in the center of Warsaw, are packed with them. If you are looking, however, for a specific type of product, the only way is to ask friends or acquaintances. The wonderful dressmaker, engraver, or jeweler may huddle in a basement in a narrow lane in the Old City or in some well-hidden courtyard.

There is a reason for the low profile of these small businesses. They are afraid that if they become too conspicuous the tax collectors will be after them. The tax structure is steeply progressive, so that it simply does not pay to grow beyond a certain size. That is why even a highly successful shopkeeper never thinks of moving to better quarters or enlarging the premises. Do not be deceived by the modest, even shabby appearance of the shop—it does not mean that its merchandise is inferior or the workmanship not up to par.

Jewelry made of amber—the semiprecious stone, actually tree resin petrified over thousands of years and found on the Baltic coast—is a specialty of Poland. Amber jewelry can be purchased in many stores, but it is particularly effective when made by an artist designer.

Handmade tapestries, called kilim, suitable for either the floor or the walls, can be had in traditional folk patterns or modern ones; entire pictures can be woven in wool. The kilims are sold abroad in the Cepelia Polish art stores, but they cost less in Poland.

Polish crystal and china are very attractive, but they are hardly the kind of thing to be thrown into a suitcase to be tossed around by airline luggage handlers.

Antiques are probably the most desirable item to be found in Poland, but their exportation is strictly controlled, unless they are purchased for hard currency in the Desa government stores, by which time they may not be bargains any more. In any case, any really old and valuable material would be barred, unless authorized by the office of the Curator of Arts.

Upscale shoppers, if not allowed to take out of the country some priceless art treasure, can always buy a pure-bred Arabian horse for a few hundred thousand dollars, as their export is encouraged. The Arabians, bred in Poland since the 17th century, are also art treasures of a kind, live ones for a change. Some of them fetch prices in the same league as French impressionist art (see Horseback Riding chapter).

Not far from Warsaw, at Milanowek, there is a silkworm farm and plant that produces beautiful silk fabrics. Its products are sold in the Milanowek store in Rutkowskiego street in the center of the city. Buying the silk fabric there and having a Warsaw dressmaker turn it into a stunning gown would cost a fraction of what it would cost in the West. As with so many other things in Poland, finding a good dressmaker is purely a matter of personal contacts. They do not advertise or even put out signs, but some are very talented, creative designers.

The shoemakers do have small shops on the street, with a display of their work in the window, so they are easier to find. They will make excellent shoes to measure, for men and women, also at a much lower cost than custom-made footwear in the West.

There are also many shops with good quality leather goods, such as suitcases, handbags and wallets. They are, of course, handmade as are all the quality articles in Poland.

Photographic equipment is not easy to get, so it is better to bring it with you. Only a few shops develop Kodak film and often take a long time to do so. If you want to have your pictures ready quickly and at less cost, use the locally available film, even though its quality may not be equal to American film.

Food and Drink

Polish cooking, traditionally on the heavy side, is getting lighter, both for health and economic reasons. In old Polish recipes butter and sour cream played an important role, as did wild mushrooms for seasoning. They still do, though in less gargantuan quantities.

A particularly good dish is chlodnik, a soup served cold, even chilled, in the summer. It owes its red color to beet roots and the slight bite in its taste to a touch of vinegar, but it has many other tasty ingredients and half a hard-boiled egg floating in the rich mixture.

Barszcz (in America, borsht) is somewhat similar, except that it is served hot, with small dumplings swimming in the red concoction, which includes many vegetables and some bits of meat.

Barszcz, as well as several other Polish dishes, is thought in the United States to be typically Jewish, but this is due to the fact that these Polish specialties were brought to America mostly by Jewish emigrants. Bagels, for example, were made by Polish Catholic peasants for centuries and in Poland are called *obwarzanki*. Gefilte fish and matzos, however, are genuinely Jewish food.

Pork chops and steaks are seen today more often than beef dishes, as beef seems to be harder to get for some reason. Wild game, such as venison, boar, or duck, is often served in restaurants, but turkey is scarce.

It is not easy to recommend restaurants in Poland. Those in hotels and the larger ones in major cities are operated by state-controlled agencies, which are not noted for creative, imaginative cuisine. The best restaurants are those run by private owners, who really try to please their customers. There are quite a few of those, but they are to be found mainly on the outskirts of town or in side streets. They are generally rather small and do not aspire to getting larger, because the state—although it tolerates private businesses to some extent—does not want them to become too important. There is no incentive to advertise when growth is not an acceptable goal. Consequently, the private restaurants rely on word-of-mouth recommendations and do quite well on that basis, within the limits of the system. This means, however, that a foreign visitor cannot find them easily, except by seeking advice among local Polish acquaintances. As in so many other areas, a friendly guiding hand is very useful and hence, the emphasis on ways of meeting people.

Some of the top official restaurants are quite good, for example, the Wierzynek in Cracow, a showpiece in a lovely ancient building with a magnificent view of the central city square and its medieval monuments. In Warsaw the restaurants of the best hotels, such as the Victoria and Forum are also good, as is the Krokodyl in Old City Square. But these elegant eating places are no substitute for the kind of charming, small family restaurants one finds in France, Italy, or Austria by the hundreds.

Some of them do exist in Poland, but they deliberately keep

a low profile. Ask your Polish friends and they will tell you where to look for excellent food and a pleasant atmosphere.

Unfortunately Poland does not have enough equivalents of the French bistro or English pub—friendly places where civilized people can share a drink in a cozy setting. There are some wine bars of varying quality, but again, one has to depend on local advice so as to avoid the wrong ones.

Speaking of drink, alcoholic beverages are one thing that never seems in short supply in Poland. There are countless varieties of vodka, with all kinds of fancy names, for example the Zubrowka, named after the aurochs (a kind of bison) of the great Bialowieza Forest, because in the bottle are a few blades of grass that grow in the forest and supposedly impart a unique taste to the liquor. The basic type of vodka is the *czysta* (pure) with the added qualifier *wyborowa* (choice). It is quite simply 45% ethyl alcohol and a bottle sells for $1.

The price of a bottle of vodka is supposed to set the rate of exchange of the dollar in the free market. If it costs 800 zlotys and the same bottle can be bought at the Pewex for $1, then the exchange rate is 800 zlotys to a buck. One need not necessarily believe that theory, current in drinking circles, but it makes as much sense as the elaborate speculations of the economists.

At the Pewex one can buy, for dollars or other hard currency, not only Polish vodka but also all varieties of whiskies, gins, brandies, and liqueurs imported from Scotland, England, France, and other countries at very attractive prices. A 0.75-liter bottle of Johnnie Walker Red Label costs $4.80, about half its U.S. price or less. Beefeater Dry Gin is $2.80 a bottle and the French cognacs are similarly priced. A can of Heineken beer is 35 cents. A bottle of Italian chianti is $1.50 and other wines are priced proportionately. (Incidentally, a pack of 100-mm American cigarettes—any of the major brands—is 65 cents.)

Polish vodkas and other liquors are even cheaper. The prices cited were current in 1987, but there is no reason to believe that they have changed much. The prices were also those of the Pewex stores, where the tags are in dollars and cents.

Price tags in the regular stores list values in zlotys. Their assortment of wines and liquors come only from "socialist" countries—at even lower prices. The wines from Hungary, Yugoslavia, Bulgaria, Rumania and the U.S.S.R. are quite good. Soviet champagne may not be equal to the best from France, but it certainly surpasses those of other countries, including the United States. It costs about $1 a bottle.

Both the government and the church are conducting campaigns against alcoholism, but they do not seem to change the fact that Poland is paradise for the serious drinker.

That is evidently the opinion of the Swedes, who in their country suffer severe restrictions on the sale of liquor and very steep prices. Fortunately there is a ferry service between the two countries, and droves of Volvos or Saabs arrive in the promised land, propelled by a keen interest in Polish culture and unquenchable thirst.

Sweet Delights

Once upon a time in New York City, someone started a chain of very select pastry bakeries called Babka. The name was a clue to the origin of the venture. Babka in Poland is a light, fluffy cake. Actually all the Babka pastry cooks were Polish, if not the owners. The art of baking in great variety has always been highly esteemed in Poland, where pastries bear little resemblance to the cakes sold in supermarkets and produced in huge factories somewhere far away.

Each Polish pastry has a personality of its own and every baker has his own individual style, appreciated by connoisseurs as a particular vintage is by wine tasters. In every Polish city—more particularly in Warsaw—scores of small bakeries specialize in choice pastry. Because the baking is done at night, people visit the shops in the morning to get the delicious *paczki* (a fluffy and fragrant ball, which bears the same relation to the doughnut as a Rolls Royce to a Yugo) still hot from the oven. There are all kinds of baked goods, with some French, some Viennese or Danish influence, but all done the Polish way. Among the purely Polish specialties is the poppyseed roll, with a taste all its own. To feed the insatiable demand for poppy seed, many Polish farmers grow fields of poppies. Although some people discovered that they can also produce opium, the drug problem has so far not reached the proportions it has in the West.

Blikle, the best known pastry shop in Warsaw, has been in business more than a hundred years. Often a line forms before Blikle's on Nowy Swiat Avenue—not that there is any shortage of pastries, but the reputation of the master bakers attracts hundreds of people. One can get excellent pastries in a wide variety, however, without waiting at Blikle's. Just go to one or another of the many bakeries in town. They are called *cukiernia*.

Ironically, the high quality, freshly baked pastry, which is a luxury sought by American yuppies—if you can find it at all in an American city—is purchased in large quantities by everyone in Poland; witness the far from affluent appearance of the customers in the local Polish bakeries. The price is reasonable even for the general population. For a foreign visitor it is almost embarrassingly low—expressed in cents rather than dollars.

Medical Services

*I*n dealing with health services, the tourist must distinguish two types of service: treatment of visitors who develop a complaint while in Poland and treatment of persons who planned to receive some before arriving in Poland.

Medical Emergencies

In case of any medical emergency, the foreign visitor can apply to any of the numerous outpatient clinics (called *przychodnia*). These clinics, staffed by physicians of various specialties, treat Polish citizens free of charge; medicine is nationalized. They also can direct a patient to a hospital, if required, or take any other necessary measures.

Foreigners are not entitled to free treatment (though they would no doubt receive it in case of a real emergency) but the fees they may be charged are only a fraction of the price of similar services in the United States. The fees may be payable in hard currency, but even then they are moderate. While the medical services are run by the government and their staffs are civil servants, they may treat patients on a private basis. In that case, they will obviously give them more attention and their fees, though higher than at the clinic, will still be far below the American level.

The problem is the shortage of many medications, that is, those that have to be imported and paid for in hard currency. The clinics would not have them, but they could be ordered from abroad if necessary. As noted earlier, persons requiring medication on a regular basis are advised to bring an adequate supply with them.

In Warsaw, information on medical services can be obtained from: The Health Service Information Center, Rutkowskiego 12, phone 26-27-61 and 26-83-00.

Treatment Planned Before Arrival in Poland

Because of the much lower cost of health care in Poland, some people plan to have certain procedures carried out in Poland.

This would not apply to major operations such as coronary by-pass surgery or other complex and life-threatening procedures. Polish hospitals are not as well equipped as American ones and some medications are scarce.

On the other hand many elective operations or procedures can be performed satisfactorily at a cost several times less than in the United States. This applies especially to plastic surgery for cosmetic reasons: varicose vein and other minor operations, at a savings of thousands of dollars.

Persons planning such treatments can contact a physician in the specialty required, discuss the problem, and agree on the terms. Names of physicians can be obtained from the Medical Information Center or from one of the outpatient clinics.

Here are the names of some doctors recommended to me as highly qualified. It is a short, random list arranged by specialty and there are hundreds of others:

Dental prosthetics: J. Hugues, Warsaw, phone 25-32-20
Dermatology: J. Suchanek, Warsaw, phone 26-25-71
Gynecology: J. Chmielewski, Warsaw, phone 45-58-81
   and Prof. Klimek (sterility), Cracow, phone 22-28-57
Internal medicine (and surgery): J. Wilczynski, Warsaw, phone 21-21-57
Pediatrics (and surgery): Prof. K. Lodzinski, Warsaw, phone 27-12-78
Plastic surgery: Ms. Z. Witwicki, Warsaw, phone 27-81-57

The addresses and phone numbers of some clinics in Warsaw follow:

Alfa Polyclinic of Medical Specialists, Ordynacka 15, phone 26-45-02 and 26-34-97
Consulting Outpatient Clinic, Walicow 20, phone 20-10-17
Dentistry, Ogrodowa 8, phone 20-23-49
Eskulap (home visits) Zurawia 24a, phones 21-80-42, 28-92-92, 28-35-35
Fast Repairs of Dentures, Al. Jerozolimskie 113, phone 29-92-97
Home Visits Polyclinic, Bracka 1, phone 28-51-01
Izis Beauty Parlors and Medical Cooperative, Al. Jerozolimskie 49, phone 21-36-19 and Marszalkowska 55/73, phone 29-34-25
Medical Clinics (outpatient), Marszalkowska 62, phone 28-39-26 and (orthodontia) Marszalkowska 140, phone 26-88-80
Medical Specialists Cooperative, Zurawia 24a, phone 28-86-92

Dentistry

*I*f you require some dental work, especially work involving dentures, the savings on having it done in Poland could pay for your entire trip, including air fare and several weeks of vacation.

This statement is not a guess or hearsay, but actual experience. It happened that when I was visiting Poland, my dental bridge worked loose and needed replacement. It was supported by two sound teeth, bridging the space left by two teeth already lost. Helped by friends, I started looking for a dentist. The idea of going to a state health service clinic did not appeal to me, as I had heard that one had to wait hours and the treatment was not always what it should be. That is why those who could afford it used dentists in private practice, in the traditional belief that you get what you pay for. I was prepared to pay up to $100, which would be a considerable bargain by American standards. Time was short, as I was about to leave and in August all the best dentists recommended to me were on vacation. Evidently their earnings allowed them to take longer vacations than the state employees.

Finally someone suggested that I try the nearest dental

clinic of the state health service, which is theoretically free—
though not to foreigners. Reluctantly, I went there since I was
anxious to have the job done before my departure. The clinic
was neat, though not nearly as opulent as it would have been
in Miami and the equipment was more modest. I did wait
about an hour, but that was not much more than I wait after
making an appointment at home.

The dentist, a youngish man, seemed highly competent.
He made molds of the jaw and the teeth still in place and told
me to return in a couple of days for the first fitting. Two such
visits were required to make the necessary adjustments. The
bridge was made of stainless metal, not gold, but it was very
smooth and seemed to fit perfectly.

Remember the dreaded moment when they tell you the
amount of the bill and stand ready to revive you if you should
faint of shock? Well, I very nearly fainted too. The bill for the
three visits and making the denture came to the equivalent of
less that $25. Feeling that he deserved better, I tried to give the
dentist more, but he declined, saying that it was the regular
price.

After returning home, I showed my bridge to an American
dentist friend and asked him what he thought of it, without, of
course, telling him where it came from. He examined the
bridge carefully and found it quite satisfactory, after which I
asked him how much it should cost. He said, "About $1,000,
but for you as a friend I could do it for only $750."

My experience may have been somewhat exceptional in
that the public clinic is not supposed to serve foreigners on the
same terms as citizens. They may have overlooked it because
though not born in Poland, I speak Polish fluently. Even if this
case was not typical, I relate it exactly as it happened to give a
scaled idea of the gap in prices in this area. The private
dentists might have charged twice or three times as much, but
even then the savings would have been enormous.

In months other than August and when one is not rushed, it

would not be difficult to find good private dentists. The dental clinic at 32 Pierwszego Sierpnia street in Warsaw (phone 46-00-54) could be helpful. As with so many other things in Poland, personal recommendations are the best way to find what you need. By the way, four years later that $25 bridge remains in place and never gives me any trouble.

If you contemplate having some dental work done, it would be a good idea to bring with you some dental supplies. Any dentist could tell you what might be needed but mainly such supplies as those used for fillings or for bonding and the like. They can be purchased in dental supply stores and require no prescription. Such materials are in short supply in Poland. By bringing them you will win much goodwill and ensure the good quality of the material used. If it should not be used on your job, it could serve as very desirable barter and certainly would not be wasted.

The Theater

The theater's role in Polish culture is quite different from its role in other countries. It provides far more than mere entertainment. It is also an educational medium and a form of ideological expression. Poland has a theatrical tradition of centuries and the names of the great actors of the past rank with those of writers, artists, and even statesmen.

Some of the greatest masterpieces of Polish literature are plays, including some dating from the 18th and especially the early 19th century, although *The Wedding*, a superb poetic drama, was written by Wyspianski around 1900. These are plays that deal not only with the loves, life, and death of individuals, but also with major issues of national existence and destiny.

That tradition is still alive and the modern Polish plays, such as those of the brilliant playwright Mrozek, are full of subtle political overtones, metaphors instantly understood by a sensitive audience.

A theater that sets itself such high goals requires directors and actors of outstanding ability. This can be achieved only within the framework of a permanent company of creative artists for whom the theater is a calling as much as a profession. They are graduates of academies of dramatic art, enrolled in theatrical companies which constitute carefully assembled teams.

Actors are permanently employed, with all the rights of public servants, as are stage designers and directors. This system is only possible, of course, because the theaters are funded by the state and do not have to depend on commercial success. It also means that if a play requires a cast of twenty, cost considerations are not an obstacle. The repertoire also is not guided by the box office. As a result classics are played regularly, as are plays that elsewhere might be considered too highbrow for general audiences.

That organization of the theater, incidentally, is not an innovation introduced by the current government. It has existed in Poland for generations. Theaters were funded before by the city; now the tradition is continued by the state on a larger scale. The directors of individual theaters have considerable autonomy in the choice of plays and their presentation.

Warsaw has about twenty theaters, which specialize in various types of shows, such as classic drama, comedy and musicals. There are also permanent legitimate theaters in all the major cities and many of the smaller towns, which elsewhere would not dream of having their own theater of high artistic caliber. For example, near Cracow, the industrial town of Nowa Huta, centered on its huge steel mill, has a first-rate theater.

The price of tickets is moderate, with discounts for students and members of various organizations. The theaters are usually filled and the audience includes all classes. Recognized as a cultural medium, the theater is as important as the schools and universities.

Do not think, however, that all Polish theaters operate in an intellectual stratosphere. The Syrena theater in Warsaw, for example, offers a cabaret-type revue. The sharp wit of Thad Drozda, the master of ceremonies and chief entertainer, might be appreciated less by foreign guests than is the bevy of gorgeous girls, invariably clad scantily and often not clad at all.

The Syrena is located at Litewska 2. Be sure to come early; the theater is always packed.

Language is unfortunately a barrier to the enjoyment of the Polish theater, except for the opera, where the libretto plays a secondary role. Warsaw's opera house, a magnificent building in the center of the city, has the largest stage of Europe. It is a rotary stage, so that the most elaborate sets can be changed instantly. The quality of the performances is excellent, while the price of the tickets is minimal. The huge size of the house makes seats available most of the time.

As for drama, foreign visitors might enjoy Shakespeare in Polish, as the plots of the plays are usually familiar. The same may be true of Moliere, the great French playwright of comedy, as well as other international classics. All are often played on Warsaw stages, for example, Pirandello, Georges Bernard Shaw, Goethe, and the Scandinavian writers.

One of Warsaw's theaters is unique. It is the Jewish theater, which plays in Yiddish and which is also funded by the state. Before the war, the Warsaw population was about 30% Jewish and there were several Jewish theaters. Now, although few Jews remain, the Jewish theater continues to perpetuate the tradition. Because few people now understand Yiddish, including the Jews themselves, the audience is provided with earphones for a Polish translation—of little help for the American visitor, but English interpreters can be obtained by previous arrangement. The Jewish theater in a small, tasteful building in the center of the city, is a fascinating remainder of the past and deserves a visit.

Speaking of spectacles, there is a good circus, which sometimes tours abroad. It also hosts, from time to time, troupes
seldom seen in the West, such as Chinese, Vietnamese, and
Russian circuses. Some of them are outstanding and thrill
audiences with extraordinary feats of skill.

In addition to the theaters with a permanent company of
actors and regular repertoires, there are many small theaters of
the off-Broadway and off-off-Broadway type. Some are run by
students, others by young actors seeking original forms of
expression.

In Warsaw, for example, there is the charming Piwnica
(cellar), at Zakroczymska 11, close to the Old City. Housed in
an old cellar beautifully converted by artistic designers, it
combines a small stage with a coffeehouse and bar. It offers a
variety of mini shows, bringing the small audience and the
performers close together. There I enjoyed an evening of Kurt
Weill songs to the lyrics of Bertolt Brecht, sung in German by
a Polish tenor who stars in the opera of Mexico City. It was a
performance which would have created a sensation in New
York City, perfect for Greenwich Village. The audience of
about fifty people was stunned by a powerful rendering of
some of Kurt Weill's best.

Incidentally, it was strange to hear a Polish actor sing in
German within a stone's throw from the Old City of Warsaw,
which was leveled by the Germans during the war and then
completely rebuilt to its original state. Evidently art helps to
heal the wounds of the past.

There are many such miniature stages in Warsaw and
elsewhere. There are also special children's theaters, which are
regular size, even if their clients are rather small. In Warsaw, at
Jagiellonska 28, there is Baj, where both puppet and live shows
are produced; Guliwer, at Rozana 16; and Lalka (doll), in the
Palace of Culture in the center of the city. Tickets may be
purchased at the door.

Cinemas

There are about forty cinemas in Warsaw. Again, language is a barrier, but it might be amusing to see an American film dubbed in Polish, especially a cowboy or gangster movie. A large proportion of the films shown are American. Films from the Soviet Union and from other "socialist" countries, most of them seldom seen in the West, are sometimes interesting because of their setting and their reflection of the life in the country of origin. The same is true of Polish films, most of which never reach the screens of western Europe or America.

Music

Poland is surely one of the most musically minded nations in the world, where Chopin is a national hero on a par with kings and statesmen. Today Lutoslawski, Penderecki, Panufnik rank high among living composers. The International Chopin Competition held in Warsaw is one of the major musical events of the world.

In Poland—mainly in Warsaw—music lovers will find a rich variety of concerts, as well as major opera companies in several cities. It is to be noted, however, that July and August are not the season for either theater or music. It is the time for outdoor sports and one should not judge the Polish musical scene by the scarcity of concerts in these two summer months. Nevertheless the traditional Sunday Chopin concerts in the Lazienki park of Warsaw, by the statue of the great composer, continue also during the summer.

Held in a beautiful sylvan setting of trees and flowers, these concerts are free and open to the public. They are usually attended by about a thousand people, every Sunday at noon and at 4 p.m.

The performers are the leading young pianists of Poland

and their music is interspersed with poems recited by the best actors. Similar free performances of classical music and poetry are also held in other cities.

For people with a deeper interest in music, aspiring to be artists as well as admirers, Poland offers great opportunities. Its many musical academies, called conservatories, maintain the highest standards and have been producing outstanding performers, conductors and musicologists for generations. They welcome foreign students and are attended by young people from all over the world. The high quality of musical instruction whether in academies or by individual distinguished teachers, is not the only attraction. Add the low cost of tuition to the low cost of living (a fraction of the cost of attending Juilliard and living in New York City) and you have a winning combination.

Music is one area in which Poland can offer world-class instruction, in an atmosphere of hereditary musicality, which is an integral part of national culture. Poland is, after all, the only country which chose a great pianist, Paderewski, as its prime minister some seventy years ago. He was a friend of president Woodrow Wilson and as popular in America as in Poland.

Polish Music Festivals

January
CRACOW

A concert series featuring soloists and symphony concerts with the participation of soloists in a program of organ compositions by the early masters and by contemporary Polish composers.

February
BIALYSTOK

Music and Poetry Festival

The concert programs of this interesting event combine music and poetry.

WROCLAW

Festival of Contemporary Polish Music

A review of contemporary Polish compositions, with the works of Wrocław composers richly represented. This is where a good many composers make their debuts.

The performers are leading Polish artists and groups as well as foreign ensembles.

A number of attractive accompanying events is held during the festival.

The festival is held once every two years.

March
CZĘSTOCHOWA

Festival of Polish Violin Music.

An interesting survey of early and contemporary Polish musical compositions for the violin, with the participation of Polish and foreign soloists.

WROCLAW

Jazz on the Odra.

Preceded by elimination contests for youth jazz groups, this competition is organized by the Polish Student Association and the Polish Jazz Federation.

April
POZNAŃ
Poznań Music Spring.
A festival of contemporary Polish music, with special emphasis on the works of young composers. The program includes symphony, chamber and choral music.

May
WROCLAW
Days of Organ and Harpsichord Music.
The festival program is composed of recitals and symphony and chamber concerts. The survey of early and contemporary compositions for organ and harpsichord features Polish and other chamber and symphony orchestras.

LAŃCUT
Days of Chamber Music.
A series of chamber concerts held in the magnificent chambers of the historical palace of Lańcut, picturesquely located in an attractive park. Polish and foreign chamber groups are featured.

June
KRYNICA
Festival of Arias and Songs.

OPOLE
Polish Song Festival.
A popular festival of Polish songs (rock, jazz, cabaret, poetic and folk) which is also a survey of performers. Leading groups and the best Polish vocalists are featured. Many attractions are offered during the festival.

POLAND

SOPOT
August

FROMBORK
July-August

GDAŃSK-OLIWA
July-August

KOŁOBRZEG-
POŁCZYN
July

KAMIEŃ
POMORSKI
July-August

BIAŁYSTOK
February

BYDGOSZCZ
September

CIECHOCINEK
June

POZNAŃ
April

WARSZAWA
September
October

ZIELONA GÓRA
September

WROCŁAW
February, March,
May, August

CZESTOCHOWA
March

OPOLE
June

KRAKÓW
January

ŁAŃCUT
May

KUDOWA ZDR.
July

DUSZNIKI
August

September
ZAKOPANE

KRYNICA
June

Music

CIECHOCINEK

Pop Concert Symphony Orchestra Festival.

Organized each year in the famous Spa, the festival of symphony orchestras is, as its name implies, a popular and ambitious event. In addition to the pop concerts there are also concerts whose programs feature the works of Poland's leading composers, preceded by introductory remarks. Leading Polish symphony orchestras are heard in this very popular festival.

July

KUDOWA-ZDRÓJ

Moniuszko Festival.

Devoted to the works of the originator of the Polish national opera and Polish concert songs, the program is widely diversified. Some of the concerts are held in the lovely park. Leading Polish performers and opera companies appear in the program.

KOLOBRZEG-POLCZYN

Festival of Military Music and Songs.

A colorful and varied program devoted exclusively to military music and songs which attracts crowds of tourists. Featured in this popular event are leading orchestras and soloists. The concerts are held in Kolobrzeg and in Połczyn, two neighboring towns.

July–August

GDAŃSK-OLIWA

Festival of Organ Music.

A series of organ concerts held at the 13th century cathedral of Oliwa. The organ is one of the most famous instruments to be built in the 18th century. Famous Polish and foreign soloists are heard in these concerts.

FROMBORK

Frombork Concerts.

Held each year at the famous cathedral of Frombork, a town where Nicolaus Copernicus, the great Polish astronomer, worked and lived and where he created his epoch-making work. The virtuosos featured in the concerts come from Poland and from other countries.

KAMIEŃ POMORSKI

Festival of Organ and Chamber Music.

One of the many Polish festivals devoted to organ and chamber music, the event is set in lovely and dignified surroundings. The concerts are held in the impressive Gothic cathedral of the 12th century, with its famous Baroque organ, and in the beautiful bishop's palace of the 16th century. The concerts attract large numbers of Polish and foreign tourists on vacation on the Polish seacoast. Featured in the concerts are Polish and foreign virtuosos and chamber groups.

August

DUSZNIKI

Chopin Festival.

In this well known spa of Lower Silesia, known as Duszniki, the young Chopin, who had come here with his mother for the cure, gave a benefit concert. In the annual Chopin Festival held in Duszniki, leading Polish and foreign pianists as well as the winners of the International Chopin Competition held in Warsaw are featured.

WROCLAW

Wratislavia Cantans.

The oratorio and cantata festival of Wroclaw has, in a brief time, risen to the rank of an international event thanks mainly to its unusually interesting program and the performers featured in it. Concerts are usually held in one of the truly impressive Gothic churches (reconstructed after the war by People's Poland). The official and highly elaborate program is enriched by a large number of highly attractive accompanying events. Wratislavia Cantans, next to Warsaw Autumn, is one of the most representative music festivals in Poland. Featured are outstanding Polish and foreign soloists, conductors and orchestras and choirs.

SOPOT
International Song Festival.
A colorful and happy accent among the Polish music festivals. It was an international event from its inception. Performing in the contest are Polish and foreign vocalists. The prizes awarded by this popular festival have launched many Polish and foreign winners on a professional career.

September
BYDGOSZCZ
International Festival of the Early Music of Central and Eastern European Countries.
Organized for the third time in 1972, the festival is devoted to the music of the 15th and the 16th century. It is one of the most interesting festivals of early music with a totally unique program. Working sessions, with the participation of famous Polish and foreign musicologists, and associated events, are held at the time. Polish and foreign groups are heard in the programs. The festival is held once every three years.

ZIELONA GÓRA
International Festival of Song and Dance Ensembles.
A review of stylized folklore featuring Polish and foreign folk amateur groups. The festival is held once every two years.

ZAKOPANE
International Folk Festival of the Mountain Region.

POLAND

The finest Polish and foreign folk ensembles are presented in the rich and brilliant review of a fascinatingly unique folk music.

WARSAW

International Festival of Contemporary Music.
Warsaw Autumn.
One of the largest Polish festivals devoted to contemporary music and one of the biggest and most important festivals of this type in Europe. The first Warsaw Autumn festival was held in 1956. At first the festival was expected to be held every two years but the immense success of the event determined it would be held yearly.
The purpose of the Warsaw festival at the time it was organized, as it is today, is to create a regular meeting place in Warsaw for all the trends in contemporary music, a place for confrontation and exchange of views and for establishing contacts between musicians of the different nationalities.
This concept was totally new from the already existing international festivals of this nature. The wide reactions it evoked and the high rank it has been universally accorded testify that the aim by which the Polish Composers Union was guided when this important and challenging event was launched has been achieved to a large degree.
Contemporary music owes a great deal to the impulses set by the Warsaw Autumn festival and Polish music in particular. The festivals instructed and inspired, they created, thanks to the excellence of the performance and the presence of foreign observers, the most desirable conditions for the start of an international career in music.
The repertory of Warsaw Autumn represents a highly objective cross-section of contemporary music as it is written today and takes account of the broadest spectrum of the numerous trends in music. Despite the fine quality of performance, it is pri-

70

marily a problem festival which is a natural result of the program.

October
WARSAW
International Jazz Jamboree Festival.
The festival provides a yearly opportunity for Polish and foreign jazz groups and soloists to meet. It draws large numbers of foreign journalists, representatives of music institutions and of concert agencies, large record firms and radio networks. It is one of the most important jazz events in Europe.

International Music Competitions

FRÉDÉRIC CHOPIN
International Piano Competition in Warsaw
Held in Warsaw every five years, the Frédéric Chopin International Piano Competition is one of the most prestigious piano contests in the world.
The contestants [below the age of 30] perform before a jury composed of leading Polish and foreign Chopinists. The program is exclusively, according to contest rules, the works of Chopin. The winners are launched upon an international career. The Frédéric Chopin Society in Warsaw organizes the competition.

HENRYK WIENIAWSKI
International Competitions in Poznań
HENRYK WIENIAWSKI
International Violin Competition in Poznań
One of the most celebrated international violin contests, held in Poland every five years.

Contestants [below age 30] who take part in the three-stage competition are expected to perform the works indicated in the rules, including the works of Henryk Wieniawski.
The concert stages of the world stand open to the winners of the contest.

HENRYK WIENIAWSKI
International Violin Makers Competition
The contest, open to professional violin makers, has won a position of international importance.
The Henryk Wieniawski Music Society of Poznań organizes the Henryk Wieniawski International Competitions.

Jazz

Jazz is extremely popular in Poland, a music-oriented nation if there ever was one. Some Polish jazz musicians acquired international reputations, playing everywhere from New York's Greenwich Village to Sydney in Australia.
The Polish Jazz Association organizes a series of events as follows:
March—tour of the principal cities by contest winners of the titles best player of each instrument and the best group of the year. The contest is organized bimonthly by the Jazz Forum.
April—finals of the Jazz Juniors, in Cracow.
May—the Old Jazz Festival, organized by the Stodola jazz club in Warsaw, an international event.
June—Jazz on the Oder (the river Oder is Poland's western boundary). The event is held in Wroclaw and is organized by the Palacyk club.
July—Jazz Workshop in Gniezno (western Poland).
August—Big Band Workshop in Bydgoszcz (western Poland).
September—"Mini Jazz" festival—solo, duet, trio—in

Jazz

Cracow; and Festival of Jazz Vocalists, international contest in Zamosc.

October—Jazz Jamboree in Warsaw. This is the major international jazz event of the year, held in the great hall of the Warsaw Palace of Culture, with some performances in the Stodola, Remont, and Akwarium clubs. It is attended by many world-class jazz artists from the United States and other countries. Because it is tremendously popular, reservations should be made months ahead, at the office of the Polish Jazz Association, Mazowiecka 11, Warsaw.

November—Jazz Expo, a show and contest for jazz posters, held in Bydgoszcz.

December—festival of jazz pianists in Kalisz; and jazz film festival in Wroclaw.

The Akwarium Jazz Club in Warsaw has a large building on Emilia Plater street, close to the Central railroad station. It has a restaurant and bar and offers daily jazz performances by Polish and international groups. Programs change weekly. It also sells posters, records, and cassettes. The Akwarium is Poland's principal jazz center and one of the first places visited by young people of many nationalities on arrival in Warsaw. It is also obviously a meeting place for all jazz lovers, young and old, or even for people with little interest in music.

Other leading jazz clubs in Warsaw are the students' Stodola and Hybrydy. Leading jazz clubs in other cities are the Rura in Wroclaw, Kosz in Zamosc, Rotunda in Cracow, and Palacyk in Wroclaw.

Information about jazz performances and special events can be obtained from the Polish Jazz Association, Mazowiecka 11, Warsaw, phone 27-79-04 or 27-21-09.

In any case the Akwarium is one of the more lively spots in Warsaw and well worth a visit.

Art

Contemporary art is, perhaps, one of the best buys in Poland. Works by living artists can be exported freely (unlike those of artists of other periods).

The problem is, of course, how to find good art—whatever that is. The exhibits at some of the top hotels, such as the Victoria or Forum in Warsaw, are mostly kitsch—perhaps in the belief that it would appeal to foreign tourists.

Art of incomparably better quality can be acquired elsewhere at less than half the price. There are many art galleries, some operated by associations and others private. For example in Sopot, the popular seaside resort on the Baltic coast, there is near the pier a large gallery, showing at all times the works of about twenty artists. Periodically the shows change, but art works are for sale at moderate prices, starting at about $30. Although the quality is uneven, several fine paintings are usually on display. Anyway, it is largely a matter of personal preference and taste.

A good place for finding some excellent work at a bargain price are the academies of art, found in all major cities. Some of the most talented students produce outstanding work. It matters little whether they are graduates or not. After all, some pictures by Picasso, which he painted at the age of 15, are considered better than some of his later work.

There are both abstract and representational paintings, with the latter in ascendence lately. The pricing of art is, of course, an art in itself. A museum of modern art in Palm Beach, Florida, recently paid $264,000 for a piece of canvas, about 3 by 4 feet painted flat black, without any pattern whatsoever. If anyone painted the same thing in Sopot, it would probably sell for $5, but then it would not be art.

Some foreign art collectors who evaluate artistic merit by their own judgment rather than price find Poland a rich source of paintings and sculptures, which they probably sell later at ten times the cost.

Graphic art (posters, illustrations, decorative pictures) has many first-class representatives in Poland. It might be interesting to acquire the originals of their work.

As in so many other fields, the best way to discover fine art is through personal recommendation and visiting the artists' studios. Looking for original talents can be at least as exciting as hunting for choice mushrooms in the woods. It is the gamble, the idea of hitting the jackpot through the work of a terrific new artist that provides the thrill. This game can, of course, be played in other countries too, but at costs in quite a different league. Think what some paintings might cost if a black background alone is worth a quarter of a million dollars. Or is it?

In Cracow the Academy of Art students display their work on the ancient city walls, by the Barbican, a fort dating from the 14th century. It's a perfect setting, with a background competing with the pictures for artistic merit—and sometimes winning.

Some Lesser-
Known Museums

*W*arsaw has about forty museums. The major ones are described in other guidebooks. A few lesser known, smaller museums, merit a visit.

For example the Muzeum Ziemi (Museum of Planet Earth), located in an elegant small palace at Na Skarpie 20/26 (phone 29-80-63), contains astounding exhibits, for example the skeleton of an elephant, discovered in the course of excavations for sewers under Leszno street, in the center of Warsaw, in 1963. It is hard to imagine elephants roaming in what is today a teeming modern capital. There is also the skull of a rhinoceros, found recently in the vicinity of Warsaw. The presence of these animals in what is today Poland proves that hundreds of thousands of years ago, the climate of various parts of the world was entirely different and that perhaps it may change again in the future.

The ancient prisons of Pawiak at Dzielna 24/26, and the Pavilion X of the Warsaw Citadel, in the northern section of the city, are grim reminders of the past, now converted to museums. Built about 200 years ago, they were used first by the tsars of Russia and then by the Nazis during World War II to hold and torture Polish freedom fighters. They are a tangible symbol of Poland's struggle for independence. Joseph Pilsudski, Poland's leader in the 1920s and 1930s, was once a prisoner in the sinister Pavilion X at the Citadel, kept to this day in its original condition.

The Maria Curie Sklodcwska Museum at Freta 16 (phone 31-80-92) commemorates the only woman ever to win two Nobel prizes (in physics and chemistry). She did so when women scientists were unheard of and opened the era of nuclear science by discovering radiation and the radioactive elements, one of which she called polonium, in honor of Poland.

Archery

Archery has been popular in Poland since 1931, when the Poles were instrumental in founding the International Archery Federation and organizing the first world archery championship. Michal Sawicki won and became the first world champion in archery—a feat that Polish archers have not repeated since. Ms. Kurkowska-Spychajowa, however, won the women's championship seven times in the 1930s and 1940s.

There are 68 archery clubs in Poland, with about 2,500 members. They welcome foreign visitors and invite them to participate in the numerous competitions held every summer and fall.

Archery Clubs

There are two archery clubs in Warsaw:

Marymont: Potocka 1, in the northern section of the city,

phone 35-77-78 and 39-85-12
Drukacz: Zieleniecka 2, phone 10-06-28

The Polish archers are short of such modern equipment as carbon bows and arrows. Any archer bringing some would become a hero.

Other archery clubs, listed by city, club name, address, and phone follow:

Cracow: Nadwislan, Koletek 20, area code 012–22-21-22
Gdansk: Gdansk, Zalogowa 1, area code 058–56-70-95
Kielce: Stella, Krakowska 374, area code 046–53-864
Kolobrzeg: Lucznik, Kasprowicza 3, area code 897–25-921
Lodz: Spolem, Polnocna 36, area code 042–26-519
Poznan: Surma, Glogowska 1, area code 061–67-13-06
Rzeszow: Resovia, Chopina, area code 817–34-764
Wroclaw: Burza, Kollataja 31, area code 071–36-243

Bridge

Bridge is very popular in Poland and there are branches of the Bridge Association in about forty towns.

The Warsaw branch holds a tournament daily; other bridge clubs hold tournaments at various intervals, once or several times a week.

A foreign visitor looking for a bridge game with the local residents, which is, incidentally, one of the best ways of getting to know them, calls the local branch. If no one there speaks English or any language known to the visitor, someone surely will be found soon.

If the guest has no partner, a partner will be found for him or her and they can enter the tournament, which is a big word to describe a friendly game among up to 100 players, in a major city, or a dozen players, in a smaller town. There is a nominal entrance fee and rather modest prizes, but what counts are the game and the fellowship. The telephone numbers are often office ones, at the place of employment of the local club secretary, who can be called from 8 A.M. to 4 P.M., which are office hours in Poland.

Bridge

The names of the secretaries listed here may change, but the telephone number will be helpful in finding the new secretary. Listings start in Warsaw. The rest of the listings are alphabetical by city.

Warsaw: Poznanska 38 m.16 (m. means the apartment number), Mr. Mojzesowicz or Mr. Zielinski, office phone 75-17-23

Bialystok: Mr. Pawluczuk, Podedwornego 14 m. 114, home phone 283-63, office phone 75-17-23

Bielsko-Biala: Lenina 31b, Mr. Bielski, office phone (9–12 A.M.) 273-75

Bydgoszcz: Dworcowa 54, Ms. Kuklinska, office phone 42-13-61, ext. 41, Mr. Kuklinski, office phone 39-03-79

Gdansk: Reymonta 8 m.4 Sopot, Mr. Pawlik, home phone 51-29-55

Jelenia Gora: Swierczewskiego 30, Mr. Ruszczynski, home phone 25-243

Katowice: Jordana 16b m.10, Mr. Swierzy, office phone 59-28-28, home phone 51-79-82

Kielce: Waligory 1, Mr. Stobiecki, office phone 21-705, home phone 45-554

Krakow: Stolarska 7, Mr. Klaczak, office phone 22-09-46, home phone 37-31-92

Lublin: Aleja Zygmuntowska 3, Ms. Fekner, office phone 23-003, ext. 21; Mr. Spocko, home phone 29-822

Lodz: Plac Komuny Paryskiej 5, room 32, Mr. Zieleniewski, office phone 33-70-10, home phone 55-71-72

Lomza: Zjazd 11, Mr. Chmielewski, office phone 24-41 or 30-60, home phone 33-15

Olsztyn: Zwyciestwa 69a, Mr. Rustecki, office phone 27-59-95

Opole: Damrota 6, Mr. Borek, home phone 33-695

POLAND

Pila: Kossaka 23, Mr. Lewandowski, home phone 255-82

Plock: Miodowa 20 m.3, Mr. Fleming, office phone 264-56

Poznan: Reymonta 35, room 29, Ms. Turzanska, office phone 60-031, ext. 54, home phone 55-486

Przemysl: 22 Stycznia 20, Mr. Terlecki, office phone 27-41, home phone 74-20

Radom: Mlodzianowska 3/5, Mr. Prazmo, office phone 211-88, home phone 295-17

Rzeszow: Pulaskiego 13a, Mr. Ferenc, office phone 35-221, home phone 35-361

Slupsk: Sienkiewicza 19, Mr. Puzynski, office phone 32-939, home phone 256-21

Tarnobrzeg: Warynskiegc 4/7, Mr. Czaykowski, office phone, 22-38-55

Tarnow: Goldhammera 5, Mr. Sobol, office phone 54-01, home phone 55-60

Walbrzych: Chopina 1, Mr. Szymale, office phone 259-97, home phone 225-36

Wloclawek: Chopina 10a, Mr. Zalewski, home phone 281-37; Mr. Sekula, office phone 753-55

Wroclaw: Laciarska 4, Mr. Neter, office phone 44-12-30, ext. 19

Zielona Gora: Chopina 19, Mr. Dziurka, office phone 72-071, ext. 5

Chess

The Polish Chess Federation was founded in 1926 and it continues its activities, organizing numerous local, national, and international tournaments. As in several other fields of international competition, Polish women seem to be doing better than the men. Agnes Brustman is currently the best known Polish world-class player, being a championship finalist.

Polish chess clubs are classified as follows: First Senior League, Second Senior League, First Junior League, and Second Junior League.

Each club can be represented in competition by one senior and one junior team of six persons each. The juniors at this time (1987) are persons born in 1968 or later, with a special class of young juniors under age 15.

The office of the Polish Chess Federation is located at Czerniakowska 126a, in Warsaw, phone 41-41-92. The Federation can provide information on forthcoming tournaments.

The local senior chess clubs in Warsaw are:

A.Z.S. (students' club): Krakowskie Przedmiescie 24
Legion: Aleja Niepodleglosci 141
Maraton: Niecala 10
Polonia: Konwiktorska 6

Other chess clubs listed by city, name, and address are:

Bydgoszcz: Lacznosc, Babia Wies 3
Cracow: Korona, Pstrowskiego 9/15
Katowice: Kolejarz, Dworcowa 8 (railroadmen's club)
Lodz: Anilana, Sobolowa 1 and Start, Teres 56/58
Lublin: Start, Swierczewskiego 22
Poznan: Lech, Marchlewskiego 142 and Pocztowiec,
    Kosciuszki 77 (post office personnel)
Wroclaw: A.Z.S., Wybrzeze Wyspianskiego 27 (students'
    club); Hetman, Dubois 18/4; and Maraton, Kuznicza 11

Foreign visitors will be welcome at all Polish chess clubs
and can enter tournaments, or just enjoy games with local
players. Language should not be a barrier, as every club is
likely to have a few English-speaking members. Besides, chess
is a game which requires little talk and could be enjoyed even
with speech- and hearing-impaired players.

Polish Dances

Not all nations have their own dances, setting out their identity as clearly as the language. Though a have-not in some respects, Poland is quite rich when it comes to dances. Unmistakably Polish folk tunes inspired composers such as Chopin, Szymanowski, and Moniuszko. Unlike the folk dances of some countries, which are relics to be found only at some infrequent folkloric symposia, traditional Polish dances are a familiar sight both at elegant Warsaw balls and at simple country weddings.

The polonaise, a stately dance which originated at the royal court, still sometimes opens the ball, not only in Poland but also at the "polonaise balls" held annually in New York and other American cities with sizable populations of Polish origin.

Incidentally the polka, popular among Polish Americans, is seldom danced in Poland, where it is believed, despite its name, to be a Czech rather than a Polish dance.

The mazur has something of its vibrant rhythm, but it is more dashing, enthralling, and picturesque. It is attended by an elaborate ritual, conducted by an emcee who executes some parts solo, with the dancers in a circle and everyone else watching. There is more abandon, reckless gaiety, and spirit in that dance than in all the rest put together, yet it has nothing of the sensual suggestiveness of the exotic tangoes, rumbas or beguines, which are also very popular in Poland.

There are also the Krakowiak, the Kujawiak and the Zbojnicki—said to be the dances of the highwaymen of the mountains in the past.

The mazur is generally not danced in night clubs, which rely on the same international music menu that is familiar all over the world.

Polish dances are presented to the world by the Mazowsze company, which fulfills a function similar to that of the excellent Mexican Ballet Folklorico. Both troupes endeavor to interpret the national spirit through the dance and succeed in doing so by raising the traditional folk dances to an artistic level, which they perhaps seldom attained in their original form. Mazowsze has toured the United States several times, but it performs regularly in Poland. It offers a magnificent performance by nearly a hundred fine artists. To miss Mazowsze on a visit to Poland would be like leaving Rome without seeing the Vatican.

For people who prefer doing to watching, there are summer courses in Polish folk dancing. Information about them can be obtained at the Polonia Society, Warsaw, Krakowskie Przedmiescie 64, phone 26-20-41.

When asked to recommend a restaurant, especially in smaller towns, people often respond, "With dancing or without?" Many restaurants offer music and dancing to their guests, particularly on Friday and Saturday evenings, but also at other times.

The music is piano, accordion, or a small band with violin and cello. The tunes are old fashioned, sometimes hits of the 1920s or 1930s, with a prevalence of tangoes, waltzes, and fox trots. There is a retro-charm in that music of an era long past, brought to life again in a provincial setting where time has stopped. When asked, "With dancing or without?" be sure to reply "with" if you relish a trip in the time machine and a chance to witness a scene that perhaps your parents would remember. Incidentally, the dancing offers excellent opportunities for striking up acqauintances with people informally. There is no better way of meeting the locals randomly, without any commitment.

Folk Art

The traditional tapestries, called kilim, are made in many
parts of the country but mainly in the Carpathian region, and
are quite original in style. They are woven of hemp and wool
that are home grown, spun, and dyed. The strength of rugs
made by hand in cottages is such that they wear through
several generations. They are often used as wall hangings to
best display their distinctive patterns, but they are sturdy
enough to be placed on the floor.

It is also possible to buy a complete peasant attire—a folk
dress would create a sensation at a fancy costume ball or some
similar occasion. There is a wide variety of dresses from
various regions, the most attractive of them for women from
Cracow, colorful and light, or from Lowicz, with broad stripes
of vivid colors. Its design was allegedly inspired by
Michelangelo's design for the Swiss Guards at the Vatican.
This is not as unlikely as it sounds, for in times past the
archbishop of Gniezno, usually a cardinal, was also lord of
Lowicz.

For bold men, the purchase of a Zakopane mountaineer's
dress might be a good investment. It has tight trousers of white

homespun with rich embroidery on the upper part of the thigh, an embroidered shirt, a sleeveless jacket, and a broad cape to cover it all. A decorative belt, a peculiar kind of hat and a tomahawk-style cane complete this striking attire.

Another interesting example of the Polish peasant's artistic sense is seen in the Easter eggs, painted in elaborate, colorful designs, which are remarkable considering how difficult it is to paint an entire egg shell so as to obtain a complete picture. They are also different in each district, so that an expert could, on seeing an egg shell many years old, tell you what village it came from.

Christmas tree decorations are another important part of the Polish folk art. In homes where tradition is respected—and there still are some—it would be considered a disgrace to place factory-made baubles on the Christmas tree. There are hundreds of varieties of Christmas tree decorations in patterns passed from one generation to the next. These beautiful works of art take weeks or even months to make, which keeps the children busy before Christmas.

Folk art is particularly developed in the mountainous region of the Tatra, where wood carving in a distinctive style has been carried on for centuries. Even the house beams are adorned with elaborate sculptures, as are roadside crosses and shrines. This tradition is kept alive by a wood carving school in Zakopane, which has produced many outstanding artists.

Original pottery is another form of folk art expression as are some types of necklaces and other jewelry.

Horseback Riding—Arabian Horses

*T*here are few areas in which Poland can claim to be top of world class. The breeding of Arabian horses is one and that is why it merits special attention.

Horses have played an important role in the history of civilization. The early Spanish conquistadors admitted, "After God, we owed the victory to the horses." Hernando Cortez was the first to bring the horse to the Western Hemisphere when, in 1518, he laid siege to Mexico with a cavalry of eighteen.

In 1540 Francisco Vasquez de Coronado took 250 horses to the Rio Grande country, ranging over Arizona, Texas, and as far north as Kansas. Some of these horses escaped and bred in the natural state. By 1570 enormous herds of wild horses roamed throughout northern Mexico, over the great prairies of Texas, Arizona, and northward to the Canadian border. The horses brought from Spain were of mixed blood, with an admixture of Arabian brought through North Africa by the Moors.

At about the same time, but unlike the Spanish horses, the Polish Arabian horses were brought directly from the desert by way of Egypt and Turkey. Zygmunt August, king of Poland (1520–1570), started a stud farm of purebred Arabian horses at his estate of Knyszyn, near Bialystok. In 1570, his master of horses, Adam Micinski, even wrote a book about Arabians.

Breeding Arabian horses in Poland has continued from the 16th century to this day, with new stallions and mares brought from Arabia by Polish noblemen who went there specifically to pick the best specimens. One of them, Count Waclaw Rzewuski (born in 1785) was legendary. He visited Arabia frequently in search of purebred horses for his stud farms of Slawuta, Antoniny, and Biala Cerkiew. Forming close friendship with the sheiks, he wore Arab attire, spoke Arabic, and was known in the Middle East as the Emir Eage-el-Faher, a century ahead of Lawrence of Arabia. His intimate knowledge of Arabia enabled him to secure the very best horses it had to offer.

Prince Sanguszko, a great horse breeder, took part in the Polish insurrection of 1830 and was sentenced by the tsar to Siberia. When he was released in 1844, he went on a pilgrimage to the Holy Land to offer thanks for his freedom, stopping on the way in Aleppo, where he purchased the famous stallion Jedran. When the viceroy of Egypt heard about it, he sent to Poland an envoy charged with buying back the stallion. In exchange he offered the splendid Eskander Pasha, which later won a gold medal at the Paris world exhibition and produced offspring of the highest quality.

The tradition of four centuries of purebred Arabian horses in Poland survived the wars and upheavals that ravaged that part of Europe. After World War I, Arabian horses were bred by members of the same families that had started the stud farms hundreds of years earlier. In 1926 the Arabian Horse Association compiled the official *Stud Book of Purebred Arabian Horses,* based on all the records accumulated through the years. The stud book, revised periodically to include additions, is recognized as the bible of the Arabian horse world.

Following in the footsteps of his ancestors, another Prince Sanguszko went in 1930 to Arabia where he purchased several carefully selected horses, among them the outstanding stallion Kuhailan Haifi. Even though the horse died in 1932, his son, Ofir, born in 1933, continued the bloodline brilliantly.

The German invasion of Poland in 1939 cost the lives of many of the Arabian horses in Janow Podlaski and other stud farms, but the Germans realized the great value of the survivors and continued the breeding of Arabians, bringing in some horses from other private estates. The Polish personnel remained in place, as the care of thoroughbreds is a highly professional task which cannot be entrusted to novices. In 1944, under the pressure of the advancing Soviet armies, the Germans evacuated the stud farm and its Polish staff to an estate in Saxony near Dresden. In February 1945, the horses and men were evacuated again by special train, under constant Allied bombing, to the estate of Nettelau, ten miles south of Kiel, where they remained until the end of the war.

With the war over, Polish officers set free from prisoner of war camps took over the horses brought from Poland, which fortunately happened to be the British zone of occupation. The Allied authorities arranged with the Warsaw ministry of agriculture the repatriation of the horses and their guardians. In the meantime, several estates where both purebred Arabians and English thoroughbreds were raised before the war resumed their operation, the principal one in Janow Podlaski.

The restoration of the breeding took time, but already in 1958 the first five Arabian mares were sold to Britain, some of them to be purchased later by Americans. They were so well appreciated that American buyers came to Poland in 1960 and purchased eight purebred horses, then came back for sixteen in 1961 and forty-three in 1963.

Sold from Janow in 1983, the grandson of the famous stallion Ofir, named Bask, attained fame in the United States, where he won a 1984 United States national championship and other prizes. His offspring also won many championships.

Since that time, the Janow Podlaski stud farm sold more than 600 purebred Arabian horses to buyers from twenty nations. Every year, in the first half of September, auctions attended by hundreds of horse lovers and breeders are held at Janow. At the annual Salon of the Horse, in Paris, the first prizes were won in 1979, 1981, and 1982 by Polish-bred Arabians, entered by their owners from various countries. In 1984 the Polish bred stallion Favor was acclaimed in Paris as world champion and the mare Arra from Janow the champion mare of Europe.

On the day preceding the Janow auction a championship contest is held, and international experts, serving as judges, select the "horse of the year."

The prices at the Janow Podlaski auctions rose as did the fame of the Polish Arabians, the best of which are now valued at several hundred thousand dollars.

The Janow stud farm also leases horses. For example, in 1976 the United States national championship contest was won—out of 122 competing stallions—by El Paso, grandson of Ofir. The stallion, still the property of the Janow stud farm, was leased for three years to Dr. Eugene La Croix, an Arizona horse breeder.

The Arabian Horse Club of America was incorporated in 1908 and its first stud book was published in 1909 in New York. Now in the United States, there are numerous stud farms, associated in statewide clubs. They advertise their stallions in special publications. Published breeding fees start at $1,000 and range upward. The horse's pedigree is listed for at least four generations back. Polish names abound among the ancestors of the leading horses.

Unlike the English thoroughbreds, which are graded by their performance on the racecourse, Arabians are judged not only by their speed but also by many other criteria, some of them purely esthetic, as they are horses of unequaled beauty.

John L. Hervey, the prominent American connoisseur of horses, wrote in 1942,

> Let it be said that there is only one class type or breed of horse and that we owe our knowledge of him as well as our debt to him to classic Greece. For it was Greece that introduced the Arab to Europe.
>
> The origin of the Arab (as we now call him) is the world's greatest zoological mystery. When we first encounter him he is already exactly the same fixed and eternal type of animal that he is today, with the sole exception that he is not quite so large. Otherwise he has remained through all the centuries, ages and cycles, to all intents and purposes unchanged. There he stands, just as he always has stood, the one and only equine immortal.

For anyone familiar with horses, more particularly Arabians, a journey to Janow Podlaski or some of the other state stud farms in Poland would be a pilgrimage as mandatory as that of the true Moslem to Mecca.

For those as yet unacquainted with the world of horse lovers, which performs its hermetic rites by rules beyond the grasp of outsiders, the Polish stud farms—steeped in tradition as they are—offer an opportunity to seek admission to the circle of the initiated.

Besides, the stud farms are all located in delightful rural settings, which would be well worth visiting even if there were no horses there.

Riding courses are available for beginners, and experienced riders can hire horses for cross-country excursions or training in the ring. There is also a program called "Vacation in the Saddle," a weeklong group ride, with stopovers arranged previously. It is a marvelous way to see the country—from horseback, with nights in country inns and picnics on the grass.

The stud farms are not all dedicated to Arabians. Some raise thoroughbreds of the English type, or cross them with Arabians. The infusion of Arabian blood has been likened to adding a divine flavor to a tasteless brew.

For those who prefer to see the horses in action on the track, there are regular horse races in Warsaw and other cities, with the usual betting. The name of the Warsaw racecourse is Sluzewiec and it can be reached easily from the center of the city by bus or taxi. It is an opportunity for seeing the Polish-bred horses for those who do not have the time to visit their natural habitat.

Information about the stud farms and the services they offer can be obtained from the Equitation Association, Warsaw, Sienkiewicza 12, phone 27-01-97 and 28-63-75, or from travel offices.

Sports Organizations

Visitors interested in sports can obtain information about the sport of their choice—opportunities for contacting local clubs—as spectators or participants by calling the national headquarters for each sport.

The following sport club addresses are all in Warsaw, unless otherwise indicated.

Academy of Physical Training: Marymoncka 34, phone 34-04-31

Alpine Club: Sienkiewicza 12/14, phone 26-69-56

Badminton: Memorial Stadium, phone 17-60-01 ext. 97, also 17-58-81

Basketball: Sienkiewicza 12/14, phone 26-22-80

Bowling (in Poznan): Czarnieckiego 9a, phone 33-41-41

Boxing: Wiejska 13, phone 27-24-29

Cycling: Plac Zelaznej Bramy 1, phone 20-46-72, also 20-28-71

Equitation (horse riding): Sienkiewicza 12/14, phone 27-68-31, also 27-01-97

Fencing: Mazowiecka 2/4, phone 26-72-71, also 27-28-25

Field and Track: Foksal 19, phone 26-73-78, also 26-84-43, also 26-63-70

Figure Skating: Lazienkowska 6a, phone 29-52-07

Gymnastics: Wiejska 17, phone 21-98-19

Ice Hockey: Memorial Stadium, 17-80-01 ext. 60, also 17-60-64

Judo: Sienkiewicza 12/14, phone 26-13-24

Karate: Memorial Stadium, phone 17-80-01 ext. 25, also 17-53-39

Kayaking: Sienkiewicza 12/14, phone 27-49-16

Lawn Hockey (in POZNAN): Stary Rynek 76, phone 520-73

Marksmanship: Chocimska 34, phone 49-84-67, also 49-54-76

Modern Pentathlon: Powazkowska 91, phone 33-56-79

Motor Boating and Water Skiing: Wal Miedzeszynski 379 (marina on the river), phone 17-44-49

Polish Olympic Committee: Frascati 4, phone 28-50-38, also 29-04-31

Rowing: Sienkiewicza 12/14, phone 26-69-88

Sailing: Chocimska 14, phone 49-57-31

Skiing: Wojcika, phone 18-62-73

Sleigh Sports (luge, bobsled, etc.): Marymoncka, phone 34-34-79-42

Soccer: Aleje Ujazdowskie 22, phone 28-93-44, also 21-91-75

Speed Skating: Memorial Stadium, 17-29-00, also 26-63-70

Students' Sports Association (A.Z.S.): Flory 3, phone 49-33-61

Swimming: Marymoncka 34, phone 35-35-89, also 35-39-83

Table Tennis: Marymoncka 34, phone 35-35-88, also
34-19-41
Tennis: Marszalkowska 2, phone 21-80-01
Weight Lifting: Marymoncka 34, phone 34-11-45
Wrestling: Aleje Jerozolimskie 99/37a, phone 21-24-30,
also 21-36-83
Yacht Club: Miedzeszynska 377 (marina on the river),
phone 17-63-11

There are also Academies of Physical Training in Cracow,
Poznan, Wroclaw, Gdansk, and Katowice.

The Naturist Movement

The naturist (nudist) movement started in Poland in the 1960s but gained momentum in 1983 and 1984. Because the country was then in dire economic straits, it was said that the naturists were trying to help the economy by saving on clothing, including swimsuits.

It was then that the naturists began to use the term "textilian" to describe people who insist on wearing some clothes at all times. Dedicated naturists scorn the textilians as Victorian prudes ashamed of their bodies and hypocritically censorious of the liberated ones.

Sylvester Marczak, a teacher from the suburban town of Otwock near Warsaw, led the movement. He organized the first naturist beach near Swidry, about 14 miles from Warsaw, on a charming river. It is still the most popular center of the movement and easily accessible by bus or car from Warsaw.

Naturism acquired a press organ in the consumer weekly *Veto*, the founder and editor of which is also a naturist. He expounds the philosophy of naturism, supporting his arguments with pictures of its more attractive practitioners. It is not known whether many converts were won, but the paper's circulation soared.

By 1987 the number of naturists in Poland grew to an estimated 100,000. The ideology of the movement perceives the absence of clothes as a symbol of freedom and a return to nature, away from the false values of convention and the rules of a restrictive society. The naturists fervently deny any erotic intent and insist that their morals surpass those of the textilians. They also passionately advocate protection of the environment and are champions of ecology.

The leaders of the naturist movement applied to the authorities for registration of an organization they proposed to call the Polish Naturist Society. The government stopped short of granting official status to such a society, but it did nothing to prevent the practice of naturism, because no law prohibits it. Textilians, especially the more conservative farmers, do not look kindly on naturism, but can do nothing to stop it.

Local authorities do not assign sites for naturist camps or beaches, which are established spontaneously by groups of naturists, usually in the vicinity of seaside resorts. They can be identified by large parasols. About forty naturist beaches now operate regularly, patronized by the same people who return every summer.

The leading seaside naturist center is Leba, a small town close to the Slowinski National Park—a world class nature reserve, noted for its moving sand dunes, large lakes, rare birds found nowhere else, and the relics of the Nazi rocket launchers of World War II. Known as the V1, they were the first operational guided missiles, the forerunners of the present intercontinental ballistic missiles. Hitler used them against London toward the end of the war, after developing and testing them in this spot in Pomerania. The adjoining Baltic beach, stretching for many miles, is the least populated part of the

Polish coast. That is why the naturists chose it as a cosy hideout. The naturist beach is about two miles west of Leba and the largest camping ground in Poland, where spaces for tents or caravans are always available. Rooms can also be rented in the town of Leba, a fishermen's harbor, where fresh fish can be purchased on the wharf and seafood is served in simple cabins. About a mile away there is a horse breeding ranch, with ample opportunities for riding. Not far away there is a vast forest in which to pick mushrooms and wild berries.

Another naturist beach is on a small island near the port of Szczecin. It is called the Plaza Mielenska (plaza means beach). It was there that Magda, a popular naturist, was elected Miss Natura '85. Her parents are also naturists. The island can be easily reached by ferry boats from Szczecin harbor. Szczecin is a large city with many hotels and restaurants. It is connected by a frequent ferry service with Denmark and Sweden, where naturism is also popular.

In 1987 the naturist movement underwent a minor crisis eagerly reported in the Polish press. One of the smaller naturist groups tried to organize its own contest for the title of Miss Natura. There was nothing wrong about that, since there is no official organization authorized to conduct such competitions. But when it became known that the promoters of the dissident contest proposed to hold it indoors, in a hotel, all hell broke loose among the naturists. They were incensed by a violation of what they hold to be a basic tenet of their creed: that nudity is only a way of expressing unity with nature, away from civilization. That is why the naturist sites are always in secluded, undeveloped spots, where the people and nature blend into one. A contest held indoors, in a hotel—inevitably with textilians around—would no longer be a communion with nature, but rather, a show and an obscene one to boot. The overwhelming majority of naturists condemned the attempt to cheapen and discredit what they hold to be a way of life, not confined to clothes or their absence, but an approach to the world at large, seeking simplicity and openness. The storm in a teacup about a beauty contest helped to clear the air.

There is also another naturist beach in Rowy, on the other side of the Slowinski National Park, but one has to bring a tent there—in keeping with the idea of avoiding developed areas.

Other naturist beaches along the Baltic coast are to be found in Miedzystroje-Lubiewo, a small resort with some facilities, and at Chalupy and Jurata on the Hel peninsula, a thin strip of land reaching out into the sea not far from Gdynia. There is also Krynica Morska near Gdansk and Uniescie close to Mielno.

In central Poland a naturist site is developing on an island on the Vistula river, near Kazimierz Dolny, an ancient town with many historic monuments, several hotels and restaurants, an old monastery, and the ruins of a medieval castle. Kazimierz attracts many artists and writers, who have summer cottages along the river. It is a two-hour drive from Warsaw.

There are scores of other naturist beaches and sites throughout the country, but they are mostly in secluded spots some distance from the nearest town or village. Information about the naturist movement can be obtained in Warsaw at the editorial office of the *Veto* weekly, at Hoza 50, phones: 21-64-01; 21-07-01; and 29-32-80. Mr. Nalecz-Jawecki, the editor-in-chief, closely follows the activities of the naturist movement.

International Friendship Societies

The numerous societies dedicated to the promotion of friendly relations between Poland and various nations are mostly sponsored by the state. Only the principal ones are listed, as they number over forty. The office addresses listed are in Warsaw.

Africa: Rajcow 10, phone 31-41-68
Algeria and other Arab nations: Wilcza 23 m.27, phone 29-66-50
Brazil: Wierzbowa 5/7, phone 27-66-50
Canada: Senatorska 35, phone 27-28-70
Chile: Rajcow 10, phone 31-41-68
China: Senatorska 35, phone 27-12-17
Cuba: Miedziana 11, phone 20-95-64

Finland: Senatorka 11, phone 26-08-46
France: Bracka 5, phone 21-52-15
India: Wierzbowa 5/7, phone 27-39-20
Italy: Senatorska 35, phone 27-28-20
Japan: Plac Starynkiewicza 7, phone 28-25-58
Latin America: Wierzbowa 5/7, phone 27-66-50
Norway and Sweden: Senatorska 11, phone 26-08-46
Spain: Chocimska 28, phone 49-83-56
Switzerland: Brzozowa 2, phone 31-25-96
Vietnam: Mazowiecka 6/8, phone 26-79-76

No Polish–American Friendship Society is listed, for obvious reasons, though there are more Poles in the United States than in all the above countries together and the Poles have more cordial relations with Americans than with any other nation.

Several countries have their cultural centers in Warsaw, chief among them: The British Council, Aleje Jerozolimskie 59, phone 28-74-01; the French Institute, Swietokrzyska 36, phone 20-12-20; and the Italian Cultural Institute, Foksal 11, phone 26-62-88.

Academic Institutions

*S*cholars, or persons with a serious interest in learning, might take advantage of a visit in Poland to become acquainted with Polish experts in their particular discipline. Such an informal international exchange could be as rewarding as the official conventions organized periodically. Foreign guests, whether professors or students, are assured of a cordial welcome by their Polish colleagues.

The following list of the principal academic institutions in Warsaw will be useful in making such contacts. There are, of course, many universities in cities other than Warsaw—foremost among the Jagiellonian University of Cracow, founded in the 15th century—but the Warsaw institutions are more accessible, as most visitors arrive in the capital first.

The Academy of Sciences (phone: 20-02-11) is not a teaching institution, but a center for research, with many divisions ranging from physics to humanities. It is housed in a magnificent palace dating from about 1820, on the main avenue of

Warsaw, the Krakowskie Przedmiescie. Its spacious conference rooms are adorned with works of art and in front of the building an impressive statue commemorates the greatest Polish scientist, Nicholas Copernicus.

The Academy of Fine Arts, at Krakowskie Przedmiescie 5 (phone: 26-92-01), trains artists and has had many distinguished graduates during its century and a half of existence.

The School of Dramatic Art, at Miodowa 22 (phone: 31-02-16), enjoys special prestige because of the unique role of the theater in Polish culture.

The Academy of Physical Education, at Marymoncka 34 (phone: 34-04-31), with a vast campus in the northern section of the city, is the center of training in all sports. It has extensive facilities.

The Medical Academy, Filtrowa 30 (phone: 25-00-51, Telex: 813929), is the leading medical school in Poland.

The Warsaw University, Krakowskie Przedmiescie 26 (phone: 20-03-81), is the leading academic center of Poland, with a faculty of distinguished scholars.

The Warsaw Institute of Technology (the Politechnika), Plac Jednosci Robotniczej 1, trains thousands of engineers and architects who are working not only in Poland but throughout the world, including the United States.

In addition to the above institutions there are also numerous provincial universities, specialized colleges, research centers and schools.

Special Interest Organizations

Visitors to Poland can broaden their knowledge of the country and establish contacts with people who share their interests through organizations concerned with their particular activities. The following list, though not comprehensive, may be of assistance. All the addresses are in Warsaw.

Actors Association: Aleje Ujazdowskie 45, phone 29-32-71
Alpine Club: Waski Dunaj 10, phone 31-56-34
Architects Associations: Foksal 2/4, phone 20-03-81
Art Photographers Association: Plac Zamkowy 8, phone 31-03-86, also 31-23-39
Boy Scouts Association; Konopnickiej 6, phone 28-92-81
Esperanto Association: Jasna 6, phone (Mr. Leyk) 27-97-42
Engineers Association: Czackiego 3/5, phone 26-74-61
Film-makers Association: Trebacka 3, phone 27-68-91
Graphic Artists Association: Nowy Swiat 7, m.6, phone 21-78-19

POLAND

Jewish Cultural Association: Plac Grzybowski 12, phone
20-05-59
Journalists Association: Foksal 3/5, phone 27-72-21
Lawyers Association: Bracka 20a, phone 27-13-45
Medical Society: Karowa 31, phone 26-63-20
Polish-Arab Association: Wilcza 23, phone 29-32-03
Polish Pen Club: Palace of Culture, phone 26-39-48
Polonia Society, for relations with Poles abroad: Krakowskie
Przedmiescie 64, phone 26-20-41
Shortwave ("Hams") association: Nowy Zjazd, phone
26-94-11
Writers Association: Krakowskie Przedmiescie 87, phone
26-84-21

Ruch International Reading Rooms

*I*n Warsaw and in other cities are many Ruch International Book and Press Clubs. They are actually not clubs but public reading rooms, where one can relax in comfortable surroundings and read an astounding variety of Polish periodicals and newspapers, as well as publications in French, English, German, Russian, and other languages. Hence the term international.

Most of the foreign publications are Communist oriented, for example, the French *Humanite*. There are also independent newspapers, among them the Paris *Monde*, the British *Daily Telegraph*, and sometimes, the American *Newsweek* and others.

The reading rooms are open to the public at no charge. In some of them, coffee or tea and pastries are served at moderate prices. On the whole, it is a valuable public service which helps people to know more about the world.

The word, "Ruch," which you will also see on all the newsstands in the country, means "movement" or "action" and is the name of a giant news distribution company operated by the state.

Health Resorts
and Spas

Poland has many spas and health resorts with mineral waters recommended by physicians for the treatment of specific disorders. The following list classifies them according to the diseases treated.

Anemia, exhaustion, convalescence: Dlugopole Zdroj, Duszniki Zdroj Iwonicz Zdroj, Jelina Zdroj, Kudowa Zdroj, Polanica Zdroj, Polczyn Zdroj, Przerzeczyn, Szczawnica, Swieradow Zdroj, Zegiestow.

Basal metabolism or mild diabetes, obesity: Busko Zdroj, Kolobrzeg, Krynica, Polanica Zdroj, Szczawno Zdroj, Swieradow Zdroj

Children's diseases: Busko Zdroj /Gorka/, Ciechocinek, Czerniawa Zdroj, Jastrzebie Zdroj, Kolobrzeg, Rabka, Rymanow, Szczawno Zdroj, Trzebnica, Wieniec

Circulatory disorders: Ciechocinek, Dlugopole Zdroj, Duszniki Zdroj, Inowroclaw, Iwonicz Zdroj, Jastrzebie

111

Zdroj, Krynica, Kudowa Zdroj, Polanica Zdroj, Zegiestow, Naleczow
Functional nerve disorders: Iwonicz Zdroj, Jastrzebie Zdroj, Kudowa Zdroj, Ladek Zdroj, Polczyn Zdroj, Swieradow Zdroj
Gastric disorders: Duszniki Zdroj, Inowroclaw, Iwonicz Zdroj, Krynica, Polanica Zdroj, Szczawno Zdroj, Zegiestow
Glandular diseases: Krynica, Kudowa Zdroj, Ciechocinek, Iwonicz Zdroj, Jastrzebie Zdroj, Ladek Zdroj, Swieradow Zdroj
Gynecological disorders: Busko Zdroj, Ciechocinek, Cieplice Slaskie Zdroj, Czerniawa Zdroj, Dlugopole Zdroj, Duszniki Zdroj, Inowroclaw, Jastrzebie Zdroj, Krynica, Ladek Zdroj, Polczyn Zdroj, Swieradow Zdroj
Occupational toxic conditions (lead poisoning, etc.): Busko Zdroj, Iwonicz Zdroj, Ladek Zdroj.
Respiratory disorders: Ciechocinek, Duszniki Zdroj, Inowroclaw, Iwonicz Zdroj, Jedlina Zdroj, Kolobrzeg, Rabka, Szczawnica, Szczawno Zdroj
Rheumatic joint, muscle, or nerve conditions; postinjury mobility deficiencies: Busko Zdroj, Ciechocinek, Inowroclaw, Iwonica Zdroj, Jastrzebie Zdroj, Ladek Zdroj, Polczyn Zdroj, Przerzeczyn, Solec Zdroj, Swieradow Zdroj
Skin diseases: Busko Zdroj, Ciechocinek, Inowroclaw, Iwonicz Zdroj, Jastrzebie Zdroj, Kamien Pomorski, Ladek Zdroj, Solec Kujawski, Swoszowice, Swieradow Zdroj Swinoujscie.
Urinary disorders: Krynica, Szczawno Zdroj

Note: Zdroj means spring.

Inowroclaw Spa

Address: Uzdrowisko Inowroclaw, 88-100 Inowroclaw, ul. Solankowa 77

The natural salt brine waters of Inowroclaw were used for medicinal purposes as long ago as the 15th and 16th centuries, but it was established as a major health resort in 1875.

One liter of Inowroclaw brine contains 318 grams of salt and its specific weight is 1.20.

Its characteristics are similar to those of the waters of Karlsbad (Karlove Vary) in Czechoslovakia, Kreuznach, Reichall, Ischl, and Salzkammergut in Austria, also Nauheim and Oeyenhausen in Germany.

Inowroclaw has all the charm of these old-time famous European spas, though some new buildings have been added recently.

113

The heavy salt brine is diluted for the baths, but each bathtub nevertheless contains about 15 kilograms of therapeutic salt, which comprises, in addition to chlorine and sodium, a wide range of trace elements which are of immense value to the immune system. There is also therapeutic mud, odorless—unlike some muds used elsewhere for treatment.

About 13,000 people undergo treatment in Inowroclaw every year. They are served by several medical centers, notably the Rheumatological, Cardiological and Gastroenterological Centers under the auspices of the medical faculty of the university of Poznan. There is also the Geriatric Sanatorium, with a Geriatric Research Center, operated by the Medical Academy of Bialystok.

The Inowroclaw Spa employs numerous medical specialists and its guests are assured of continuous professional attention.

Inowroclaw is particularly recommended for rheumatic diseases, arthritis, postoperative conditions, joint inflammation, spine disorders, and all degenerative conditions. It also treats circulatory system complaints, especially rehabilitation after cardiac incidents.

Digestive problems, notably gallbladder and gallbladder duct ones, chronic liver and pancreas disorders, as well as obesity, are treated.

Spa treatment, of course, is not intended for acute cases requiring hospitalization. Rather it is used as a preventive measure or for convalescence. It proves to be very effective in the treatment of chronic conditions; the relaxed and pleasant atmosphere of spa life contributes as much to good health as the mineral waters.

The nearby town of Inowroclaw has a theater, five cinemas, a museum, libraries and magazine reading rooms, swimming pools, tennis courts, concerts and discotheques.

Among the sites worth visiting in the vicinity are Kruszwica, one of the oldest towns in Poland, with histoic monuments dating from the 10th century. It was there that the realm of Poland was born a thousand years ago. There are also the fascinating excavations of Biskupin, a village which existed about two thousand years ago, in prehistoric times. The city of Torun, the birthplace and home of the great astronomer Nicholas Copernicus, is not far away. Another important health resort, Ciechocinek, is also close to Inowroclaw.

Foreign guests can reserve rooms in the establishments operated by the spa administration on terms that include not only full board, but also all the facilities of the spa and medical services. The cost is a fraction of that charged in similar health resorts in western Europe. It is also possible to rent rooms in a boarding house and use the spa facilities as a guest, in which case the cost would be even less. Reservations are necessary, especially in the summer season.

Cieplice Hot Springs

Address: Zespol Uzdrowisk, 58-560 Cieplice, ul. Mireckiego 4

The Cieplice hot springs, in a mountainous part of Silesia 1,000 feet above sea level, were known in the 13th century, when prince Bernard, of the house of Piast, granted them to the Joannite Order of Hospitaliers. The deed was dated 1281 and the healing powers of the hot springs were recognized at that time.

In 1381 a Cistertian monastery was built at Cieplice and the monks operated a health establishment with cabins surrounding the springs. The spa was visited by many eminent guests, among them queen Mary, the French spouse of the King of Poland, Sobieski, who spent some time at Cieplice with her court in 1687.

One of the oldest health resorts in Europe, in continuous operation for seven centuries, Cieplice has been developed in recent years and can now accommodate a thousand guests.

There are eight springs, with water temperatures ranging up to 73° C. The waters are used in baths and also orally. They are recommended for rheumatic, orthopedic, neurological and gynecological conditions.

The drinking waters are particularly effective in urinary problems, kidney diseases, and calcium deficiencies. Cieplice water is also available in bottled form and sold under the brand name Marysienka, the nickname of the queen who visited the springs three hundred years ago.

Cieplice Spa has a theater, several cinemas, a concert hall, coffeehouses, and a guests' club. The surrounding country is picturesque, with mountains, waterfalls, and scenic paths.

Krynica SPA

Address: Uzdrowisko Krynica-Zegiestow, 33-380 Krynica, Kraszewskiego 1

*P*erhaps the leading Polish health resort, Krynica, is located in a scenic valley of the Sudeten mountain range 1,800 feet above sea level. The healing characteristics of its mineral waters were known in the 18th century and the first spa buildings were erected in 1807. The spa developed throughout the 19th century and still maintains a Victorian character with its large, ornate houses with terraces and balconies (now used mostly as boarding pensions). More recently a vast hall with an area of 45,000 square feet was built. It is called the Pump Room because waters from various springs are available there directly from the source, pumped to fountains from which people can drink them on the spot.

Krynica Spa

The carbonated alkaline acidulous waters from the Jan spring and the acidulous waters with sodium bicarbonate and iodides, as well as waters containing boron from the Zuber spring, are among the most effective, but there are several other springs with waters of various mineral content.

The treatments include mineral carbonic acid and gas-bubble baths, dry gaseous baths, hydrotherapy, vibratory massage, electrotherapy, actinotherapy, heat treatment, ultrasound treatment, and others.

The spa has a well-equipped diagnostic center and analytical laboratories. Several medical academies have research centers in Krynica and the guests of the spa are assured of continuous medical supervision by qualified specialists.

One of Krynica's major attractions is its scenic setting—the large park highlighted by the Park Mountain overlooks the village. A cable tramway provides easy access to the mountain peak with its splendid panoramic view. Winter sports can be enjoyed on the many slopes and skating rinks; in the summer, swimming pools and tennis courts are available.

Jan Kiepura, the famous Polish tenor of the 1930s and 1940s loved Krynica and his name is associated with it. Before the war, Kiepura built the elegant hotel Patria there. He owned it until the German invasion. The Krynica theater annually holds the Jan Kiepura Festival of arias and songs, in memory of the great artist.

At other times the theater presents a repertoire of dramatic plays and musicals. There are also several cinemas and many restaurants with dancing and entertainment. Daily concerts are given in the Pump Room.

Tours are organized to nearby Zakopane, the spas of Szczawnica and Zegiestow, which are smaller than Krynica, but recommended for some complaints. A particularly exciting excursion involves rafting down the Dunajec, a white-water mountain river running through a beautiful gorge. Other excursion goals are the nearby mountains, such as

Jaworzyna (3,300 feet), Huzary (2,500 feet) Krzyzowa (2,300 feet), and the Czarny Potok waterfall.

The Krynica waters are recommended for gastric and urinary conditions, cardiovascular disorders, gynecological diseases, diabetes and other chronic conditions.

Although many modern buildings were recently erected, Krynica maintains the charm of an old-world European resort steeped in tradition. In addition to the official buildings of the spa administration, which house hundreds of guests, there are several hotels and private guest houses in the sumptuous residences of prewar affluent families. They vary widely in quality, but some may offer a pleasant setting and good cuisine at moderate prices.

Some American medical insurance institutions refund the cost of treatment in foreign spas, if deemed necessary. This would apply only to bills from the spa administration, not from the private hotels. These bills include the cost of treatment as well as room and board. Check with your insurance institution. The cost of treatment in a Polish spa, even if payable in dollars, will be very much less than in an American or western European resort.

The Masurian Lakes Region and the Wolf's Lair

*T*he rivers, lakes, and canals of Poland constitute a vast network of waterways, over which one can travel hundreds of miles by kayak, houseboat, or sailing yacht. The most attractive region for such cruising is that of the Masurian Lakes, in the northeastern part of the country. There, hundreds of lakes lie amidst wooded hills, their beauty still largely unspoiled. Some of the lakes are big ones, with the other side beyond the horizon, others wind their way in valleys and ravines carved by the glaciers of thousands of years ago. They are connected by rivers and canals—a labyrinth of waterways bordered by forests. It is a region with very little industry and its hills are not particularly suited for agriculture, so there are still large natural spaces untouched by the blessings of civilization. Yet it is not a wilderness, as hamlets and villages nestle here and there by the shores.

Pleasure boats and hydrofoils cruise some of the Masurian lakes and their waterways in scheduled services and excursions. There are few hotels or inns in the Masurian Lakes region, which is favored mostly by young people using the numerous camping sites or the cabins of their boats for shelter. There are thousands of small yachts cruising the rivers and lakes, but overcrowding is not yet a problem.

Kayaking is a very popular and there are several kayak trails equipped for a downstream trip, with facilities for portaging the boats by land. The trails are provided with hostels or camp grounds spaced so as to provide shelter after a day of cruising downstream. One of the more popular kayaking routes, the Czarna Hancza, is described here separately. Cruising the waterways is a leisurely activity and a trip may take a week or two of relaxed drifting across a land of scenic beauty, far removed from the turmoil of cities.

The Wolf's Lair

Yet it was not always at peace. It was here that the Germans and Russians fought the memorable battles of World War I described by Solzhenitzyn in his great work. It is also here that Hitler had his headquarters during World War II. The historic spot known as the Wolf's Lair—the bunker which housed the supreme command of the German armies in World War II— has been preserved though it was damaged. This grim monument was Hitler's wartime home, a huge compound of giant bunkers with walls of concrete ten feet thick, designed to resist any enemy attack. When the Germans were compelled to retreat toward the end of the war these fantastic structures were blown up with dynamite, but no explosion could destroy them completely. What was left is a surrealistic world of artificial rocks and ramparts, caves and gigantic walls, with some bunkers still intact and others broken up in grotesque shapes. It is a setting for a saga of the Nibelungen, with the evil spirit of its master still tangibly present.

This was the scene of what was perhaps the most dramatic event of World War II, which could have changed the course of history. Here an attempt was made on Hitler's life by staff who believed he was leading Germany to disaster. If the Fuehrer had not walked away from the briefcase containing a bomb on July 20, 1944, the German generals would have negotiated a separate peace, with consequences that could have altered the present face of the world.

A documentary film of the period when Hitler was master of the Wolf's Lair is shown to visitors. It was compiled from the actual film records of the Wehrmacht and brings to life that extraordinary era at the very spot which was its nerve center.

Few places in the world, if any, carry a more crushing load of emotion or evoke a more overpowering image than the Wolf's Lair—the more so as its story is relatively so recent. No one who has seen it is likely to forget it, a wonderful setting for nightmares.

The Czarna Hancza Kayak Trail

One of the best known kayak trails is that of Czarna Hancza (czarna means black; Hancza is a name). It starts at Hancza Lake, close to the Soviet border, in the northeastern corner of Poland. Incidentally, the frontier between Poland and its eastern neighbor is very strictly guarded on the Soviet side with barbed wire, watchtowers, and everything to make unauthorized crossing impossible.

The Czarna Hancza river runs a sinuous course south, until it passes through the center of the small town of Suwalki, passing a few villages on the way. The country is picturesque, with heavily wooded hills climbing up to 800 feet. After Suwalki, the river crosses the Wigry National Park, a forest of many thousands of acres, maintained in its natural state. It then enters to the narrow end of Lake Wigry, which has a convoluted shape with many jutting peninsulas, islands and inlets, as well as connected satellite lakes. Lake Wigry runs from north to south and connects with several rivers south of it. Czarna Hancza continues southeast and then joins the Augustow Canal, built in the 18th century to connect the basins of the Vistula and Niemen rivers, thus linking Poland and Lithuania. The canal runs through the vast Augustow forest, which borders the Soviet frontier in the east. Turning west along the canal, we reach the town of Augustow, after passing across several lakes. The canal then runs south and connects with the rivers of the Vistula basin.

The Czarna Hancza kayak run could take about a week, or more if stops are made along the way. It is a favorite route, as it crosses a part of the country which is not industrialized and where the terrain has remained largely unspoiled. Consequently the waters of the rivers and lakes are clean, which unfortunately is not the case in other regions.

A country seen from the water side presents an entirely different picture from that observed from a train or a highway. The rivers reach secret nooks without any roads, parts that have not changed in centuries, and sleepy villages that no one would think of reaching by land. The trail of the Czarna Hancza opens a small world of beauty and mystery. It is not a trip to be undertaken individually—not that there is any danger; there is none—but because the vast network of waterways permits many variations of the route, which require someone familiar with the twists and turns of the rivers and lakes.

That is why a group of a dozen or more kayaks is usually organized, which makes for good fellowship with nighttime singing by the camp fire. There could be no more pleasant excursion for anyone ready to rough it a bit.

The Krutynia Kayak Trail

One of the more attractive kayak routes in the Masurian Lakes region is that of Krutynia, which starts in Lake of Warpuny, close to Mragowo, and continues across 18 other lakes, terminating in Ruciane Nida, at Lake Nida.

Group cruises usually start at Sorkwity, about seven miles downstream from Warpuny, from which individual kayakers can start. The route takes about nine days and the hostels are spaced accordingly. Three portages are necessary between Sorkwity and Iznota. The trail crosses Lakes Lampasz, Dluzec, Biale, Gant, Zyzdroj Wielki, Zyzdroj Maly, Zdorzno, Uplik, Mokre, Beldany, and Nida, as well as several smaller ones. It is a scenic route through the vast Piska forest, along the Krutynia River, but mostly crossing the numerous lakes connected by the river. The wooded, hilly country is not densely populated and the forests are preserved in their natural state. The water of the lakes and rivers is clear, as pollution has not yet ravaged that part of the country.

The Krutynia Kayak Trail

The trip down the Krutynia and across eighteen lakes could be an unforgettable experience. Though there is no over-crowding, one is likely to meet other kayak addicts. Poland has 180 kayak clubs, 130 sailing clubs, and 70 snorkeling clubs and there is still room for everyone in the hundreds of lakes and along the Baltic coast. Unfortunately some of the main rivers, such as the Vistula, are victims of industrialization, as is the case in other European countries. This makes the land of the Masurian lakes, with its largely unspoiled nature, all the more precious. To explore that part of the country one should go to Mragowo, which has several hotels and serves as a center for excursions by land and water.

Hunting

I am told that Poland is a great hunting country, but I would never dream of being an accessory to the murder of innocent hares, deer, or boars. The subject is closed. I can give you, however, a delightful substitute for the slaughter of the forest dwellers. It offers all the same attractions of a sylvan setting, companionship in the chase, and the sense of bringing home ingredients for a tasty meal.

Mushroom picking in the woods is an old Polish custom and has been celebrated by great poets as the ultimate rustic pastime and sport.

They are, of course, wild mushrooms quite different from the standard white mushrooms raised commercially. There are many varieties, which can be served fried, cooked in cream, or as flavorful ingredients in other dishes. The trick is to know which mushrooms are edible and which are not; there are also some poisonous ones. Most Polish people, trained in mushroom hunting from childhood, tell them apart with ease. Here, as in so many other situations, local friends are a must.

There is an element of chase and gamble in mushroom hunting, the thrill of discovering a whole colony of a particularly valued variety, such as the rydz—a copper-colored mushroom indescribably delicious when sautéed in butter. The wild mushrooms of the forest can also be pickled or dried. Then their powerful fragrance makes them the hardest substance to smuggle anywhere.

Should the pickings prove scarce, which is seldom the case, mushrooms provide the perfect excuse for roaming the woods in a group, finding new paths and clearings, meeting the animals face to face without threatening them, and having a wonderful time—with a picnic thrown in. There are lots of forests all over Poland; some are classified as national parks, others are more or less open. Rules against lighting fires and scattering rubbish must, of course, be observed.

Mushrooms, both wild and cultivated, are a very important ingredient in Polish cuisine. One can buy in the streets, for pennies, long rolls with toasted mushrooms, called zapiekanki. They certainly beat hot dogs for flavor and fragrance.

The best season for mushrooms is the late summer and fall, especially after it rains.

The Fruits of Forests and Gardens

Fruits and vegetables acquire a different flavor in Poland, perhaps because some of them are still grown in the wild or, at any rate, without artificial fertilizers. They are also very fresh, being sold usually within a few miles of their origin instead of thousands of miles. This means that they do not have to be picked half ripe to be fit for transportation.

Polish strawberries are a major export item and are considered to be among the best in Europe, but they are at their best when sold from a wayside basket. Discriminating taste is displayed by naming garden strawberries *truskawki* and wild strawberries *poziomki*. The same fine distinction applies to sweet cherries *(czeresnie)* and sour cherries *(wisnie)*.

Best of all are the wild berries of the woods. In many varieties and colors, they are picked by farmers' children and often sold at the nearest market or by the roadside at ridiculously low prices.

While the fruits from the woods are particularly delicious, there are also vast apple, pear, and plum orchards. And many Polish roads are lined on both sides by cherry trees.

Vegetables grown in gardens also have a taste and flavor superior to those grown on vast plantations. Radishes have a tang and bite often missing elsewhere, and cucumbers have a bouquet all their own, not a bland, watery taste. A familiar sight in the Polish countryside, especially in the vicinity of towns, are the rows of hothouses in which vegetables grow year-round. Their owners are reputed to be the most prosperous people in the country, their products always in great demand.

Skiing

Although Zakopane in the Tatra mountains is the uncontested center of skiing in Poland, it is by no means the only one. Actually it is usually overcrowded in the winter season and its fifty-year-old cable cars can hardly cope with far more passengers than they were intended for in 1936.

There are numerous smaller winter sports centers all along the Carpathians, especially in the western section bordering on Silesia. The mountains are not as high there as the Tatra mountains—about 5,000 feet above sea level—but they are very picturesque. Neither the Tatra nor the other Carpathian ranges can compete with the Alps, so if you are looking for almost vertical slopes starting at 8,000 feet you may be disappointed. If, however, you have yet to win a gold medal in downhill racing in Chamonix or St. Moritz, you will enjoy wonderful skiing in many winter sports stations along the Carpathians. They may not match Davos or Cortina d'Ampezzo for glamour, but they offer a warm, friendly atmosphere at a fraction of the cost of the Alpine capitals of the skiing world.

These winter sports stations are too numerous to list here,

but information about them can be obtained at the headquarters of the Polish Ski Association. The address is: Zwiazek Narciarski ulica Wojcika, 03-713 Warszawa, phones 18-62-73 and 28-44-71, ext. 110.

Snow starts in November and conditions are usually good most of the time, with snow on the northern slopes until April.

For those who regard skiing primarily as a spectator sport, Zakopane is a must, as it's there that all the major championship competitions are held with international stars participating.

Ice Sailing and Other Winter Games

*T*he frozen surfaces of many lakes and rivers make splendid tracks for ice sailing, an exciting sport. The ice yacht is rather like a catamaran with ski-like slides instead of slim hulls. Much depends, of course, on the condition of the ice and not all lakes are suitable for sailing in the winter. If the ice is smooth and free of obstacles, speeds of more than fifty miles an hour are possible.

Ice-sailing races are held on some lakes, especially in the Masurian Lakes region and in Pomerania. Some stretches of river also make good racing tracks.

Ice sailing is sometimes combined with winter fishing (through air holes in the ice). Another winter sport, requiring no slopes, is skijorring (a Scandinavian term, pronounced "yorring"), that is skiing in tow by a horse. It requires somewhat less effort than cross-country skiing, but possibly more skill as the horse can easily negotiate obstacles which may knock over the skier.

Horse-drawn sleighs are used widely in the winter and in Zakopane they function as cabs, with the driver in the traditional attire of the mountaineer. You may be surprised when the cabbie in a colorful folk costume addresses you in pure American slang—the people of the Carpathian highlands emigrated to the United States in larger numbers than those from other provinces. Some of them return and occasionally may wear the dress of a Tatra mountaineer.

Sailing Along the Baltic Coast

While ships of 100,000 tons and more are built in the huge shipyards of Gdansk and Szczecin, several smaller shipyards along the Baltic coast are busy turning out sailing yachts of all shapes and sizes, many of them for export. Some, the smaller ones, are used mainly on the lakes, especially those of the Masurian region, which used to be known as East Prussia when it was under German rule.

Other yachts set no limits on their reach and sail all the oceans of the world. The first solo Atlantic crossing on a Polish yacht was that of Bohomolec, in the 1930s.

When the "tall ships" assembled in the New York harbor for the bicentennial celebration of the United States in 1976, the training ship of the Polish navy *Dar Pomorza*, a majestic three master, was there with about sixty midshipmen on board. It was escorted by a score of Polish yachts with crews of five or six, which sailed out of Gdynia for the occasion. When Australia celebrated its bicentennial in 1988, the Polish sailing ships and yachts were there in full force.

Sailing Along the Baltic Coast

Opportunities for sea sailing out of Polish ports are unlimited, the attraction being for foreigners—as in many other sports—a cost which is a fraction of that in most other countries.

One can charter or buy a yacht, or perhaps join a Polish crew planning a cruise, which seems the easiest way.

The places to go looking for such connections are the coastal towns and villages, yachting clubs and marinas along the Polish coast, starting from Szczecin in the west to Gdansk in the east. Szczecin itself is a busy port and a city of 400,000 inhabitants. It is located inland, in the estuary of the river Odra, which is Poland's western boundary, but at the outlet of the bay there is Swinoujscie (a good name for practicing Polish pronunciation), an attractive seaside resort. Many fine beaches dot the coast, but the temperature of the water is generally more like that of Maine than Florida. Szczecin, a very old city, suffered heavy damage in the war. It was largely restored as was the massive castle of the princes of Pomerania, dating from 1346, with sarcophagi of the princes in its vaults. There is now also a theater, a cinema, and a concert hall in the vast building.

If you are touring along the coast looking for yachts, you can hardly overlook the church of Virgin Mary in Stargard Szczecinski, some twenty miles east of Szczecin. That gothic masterpiece, 250 feet in length, also has a belfry 250 feet high. The church seems out of proportion to the small town, but Stargard had its days of glory—first mentioned in records in A.D. 1124. It was granted a city charter in 1253 and competed for primacy with Szczecin as a member of the Hanseatic League. Such a port deserved a magnificent church, for medieval city fathers competed with their rivals by the height of their church spires, exactly as American cities compete today by the height of their skyscrapers. Try to beat St. Mary's of Stargard, if you can.

About fifty miles north, on the coast, stands Kamien

Pomorski, which became the seat of a bishop in 1176 and now has only 6,000 inhabitants. Its pride is a magnificent organ. Dating from 1669 and one of the best in the country, it is used in the summer months for recitals by leading Polish and foreign organists.

Further east, after some fishing villages, is Kolobrzeg, now a town of some 36,000. In A.D. 1000 the seat of a bishop, it is also the leading health resort on the Baltic coast and a minor port just right for smaller craft.

After more fishing villages we come to Darlowo (13,000 population) which has, of course, a 14th century castle and a parish church built in the 14th century but altered in the 15th and 16th centuries. There are many other medieval buildings and a somewhat more recent historic relic: the test site of the World War II German rockets, where the V1 and V2 missiles were developed. A monument commemorates the 4,000 prisoners of war who labored in the missile center and who lost their lives in a nearby concentration camp.

Relics of the Middle Ages seem to obstruct the search for yachts, so I will not mention the castles and churches between Darlowo and Gdansk. This is the hazard of traveling in a country with a 1,000-year history. Wherever you go there is some marvelous monument built no later than the 15th century. They are all described much better in other guidebooks.

The next port is Ustka, which has a small shipyard that makes all kinds of boats with engines or without. There is also a smokehouse for fish—smoked eels are the specialty. Ustka (now 13,000 population) was a Hanseatic port in the 14th century.

About forty miles east lies Łeba, a small fishing port (founded in 1357), that faces the sea on one side and a 20,000 acre lake on the other—actually an inlet separated from the sea by a narrow strip of land. Łeba is noted for one of the most popular nudist beaches on the coast.

About thirty miles east of Leba the coast takes a sharp turn south, while a slim but quite long peninsula continues due east. The Hel peninsula forms the bay of Puck, a port and small town (founded 1346) which was a base of the Polish navy in the 16th century. The village of Hel at the tip of the peninsula is also very old, with fishermen's cottages in Dutch style, perhaps built by settlers from the Netherlands a couple of centuries ago.

The bay of Puck, sheltered from the open sea by the Hel peninsula, is perfect for sailing smaller boats. A few miles south of Puck is Gdynia, one of Poland's major ports, the other two being Gdansk and Szczecin. For a change from all the preceding cities and ports, nothing in Gdynia is more than sixty years old. It is a new harbor built in the 1920s and 1930s, which became in 1937 the leading Baltic port, not in terms of Poland alone but, in terms of cargo handled.

Naturally there are hundreds of yachts in Gdynia, which forms together with the seaside resort of Sopot and the city of Gdansk what is called the "Tri-City," since the three merge into one urban unit, served by an electric commuter rail line along the coast. Trains run every few minutes.

Gdansk is a city of half a million, which existed as early as the 10th century as a coastal fort and which has a rich history. It merits a separate chapter and is described in detail in many books.

Looking along the Baltic coast for yachts in which to sail the oceans is a rewarding experience even if one should fail to find any, which is unlikely. The ancient fishing villages and towns of Pomerania are well worth seeing even if one were to ignore the hundreds of sailing and motor boats at their wharves.

Interstar Yachting Inc., 00-545 Warsaw, Marszalkowska 66 m. 24, phone 21-44-47, Telex 817577, handles yachting sales and charters, but it's more fun looking for them along the coast.

139

The Tatra
Mountains

Zakopane is the starting point of excursions into the Tatra mountains, which are certainly one of the most picturesque and attractive parts of Poland. It is seldom necessary to engage a professional guide, as in most cases acquaintances from the hotel will be ready and willing to guide a foreigner. Besides, there are many beautiful valleys and climbs in the Tatra near Zakopane, so safe that all save total invalids can enjoy them on their own, adding the thrill of exploration to the other joys of mountaineering.

If it is a matter of going for high climbing on an Alpine scale, the Towarzystwo Tatrzanskie (Tatra Society), which is Poland's Alpine Club, will advise and help prospective climbers. The Tatra mountains offer many challenging climbs, which take their toll in lives and that is why professional guidance is necessary.

The Tatra highlanders are a strongly individualistic tribe. They wear a peculiar, very striking garb and have customs of

140

their own, partly inspired by traditions handed down from the time when highway robbery was an honored profession among mountaineers. Of course they no longer practice this long lost art, merely wild songs, tomahawk dances, and other manifestations of high spirits.

Summer in Zakopane is very sunny but never hot—there is always the opportunity to dip in one of the High Tatra lakes, ice cold, but so clear that the rocky bottom can be seen at a depth of twenty feet. For those who prefer something warmer, there are the natural hot springs of Jaszczurowka on the outskirts of Zakopane. If that is not enough, there are many bars and cafes, more or less on the Warsaw model, with the artistic type well represented.

The beauty of the Tatra scenery and the keen esthetic sense of its people have been attracting numerous artists since Zakopane was discovered some eighty years ago. They set a fashion and the cafes of Zakopane still have a somewhat Bohemian atmosphere.

In the winter, dancing is the recognized warming-up method, said to be more popular than all the other sports together.

In the mountains, there are many tourist inns more spartan as the altitude increases. The best known is on the Hala Gasienicowa, at about 4,500 feet, where it is possible to establish a provisional base for several days of climbing or skiing.

The annual ski championship competition is the highlight of the Zakopane season, when the town assumes a festive aspect for several weeks and everyone prominent in Poland must be there. Nobody moves otherwise than on skis, even if the goal of the journey is no farther than the nearest bar or cafe. It is evidence of a sporting spirit, just like strolling down the main street with heavy coils of rope on your shoulder and spiked boots on your feet—in the summer, of course.

In winter all the snow sports so far invented are included in the program, with horse and motor races on ice thrown in. Perhaps the most spectacular of all is the ski jump, with men flying as much as 200 feet in the air.

Zakopane's enormous popularity may be its weak spot, for the only two cable tramways, the Kasprowy (about 5,000 feet) and the smaller Gubalowka (about 3,500 feet), are over-crowded and long waits are common. Rooms are also sometimes hard to get, though that would not be a problem for people with hard currency. Zakopane and the Tatra mountains are just as attractive in the summer as in winter, perhaps more so. Though far smaller than the Alps, the Tatra mountains have the same rugged beauty and a definitely Alpine character. They are a part of the Carpathian chain, which runs the length of Poland's southern border, with Czechoslovakia—actually Slovakia—on the other side.

Though not as dramatic as the Tatra, the other sections of the Carpathians are also well worth seeing for their scenic beauty and winter sports. The many Carpathian resorts are less crowded—and maybe somewhat less lively—than Zakopane, but they also have much to offer.

The Ojcow National Park

Only about 15 miles from Cracow is the Ojcow National Park, not the largest in Poland (40,000 acres) but perhaps the most attractive and interesting. Its hills, up to 1,400 feet high, are of calciferous rock and the rivers Pradnik and Saspowka have deep canyons or ravines bored in them as well as a vast labyrinth of underground caves. The limestock rocks take strange shapes. One of them is known as the Mace of Hercules. Many varieties of bats inhabit the caves, which have served through history as hideouts for rebels or freedom fighters.

For some reason, which still puzzles naturalists, this relatively small area contains an extraordinarily varied assortment of plants and animals, some of them not found anywhere else in the country. The hills are covered by a thick forest of beech, fir, hornbeam, oak and maple, with a variety of brushwood, including the dwarf birch, unique to the Ojcow woods.

The natural beauty of the scenery, enriched by the vegetation, offers a magnificent setting for the historic relics found in the Ojcow National Park.

The castle of Pieskowa Gora, built in the 13th century and greatly enlarged by king Casimir the Great in the 14th century, is a splendid example of medieval architecture, with ramparts, towers, and dungeons. It has been restored to its original condition and now houses a museum. In the courtyard there is a well so deep that one waits several seconds to hear the tinkle of coins hitting the bottom. In the upper chambers, works of art from the royal castle of Wawel in Cracow are on display.

One of the chambers has a secret: its acoustics are such that whispers from one corner of the huge hall can be clearly heard in the opposite corner. It seems that a prince who was lord of the castle centuries ago had it specially designed in such a way so that he could know what his courtiers, thinking they could not be heard, were saying about him.

There is also a museum of natural history with examples of the rare flora and fauna of the region, stuffed animals, the bones of species long extinct, and other fascinating exhibits.

The caverns of the Ojcow have never been fully explored, as they extend far and would present a serious danger to casual spelunkers. Several caverns, however, are open to visitors, notably the King Wladyslaw Lokietek Cave in which the Piast prince was reportedly hiding when he was struggling for the throne of Poland in the early 14th century. He finally achieved his goal and reigned from 1320 to 1333.

Beauty of nature combined with architectural masterpieces steeped in history make the Ojcow National Park a unique spot and an unforgettable experience.

The park is easily reached by bus or car from Cracow, about half an hour's drive away.

The Bialowieza Forest

*H*istory books tell us that Poland was never settled in its early years by alien invaders, as Spain was by the Moors, Russia by the Tartars, and the Balkans by the Turks. What was the reason for this immunity in the formative period of the nation, when its population was still sparse?

It was really very simple: the plain which is now Poland was then one huge forest, with only a few settlements by the rivers. That thick forest constituted an impenetrable barrier at the time, and that is why the great migrations of the early centuries of our era bypassed the territory which is Poland today, leaving it to its original dwellers who had lived there for thousands of years.

Fortunately a portion of that primeval forest survived to this day. The part in Poland comprises 226 square miles (145,000 acres) and the rest—at least as large—is now in the Soviet Union but belonged to Poland until 1945.

The Bialowieza forest was the scene of many historic hunts,

such as that of king Wladyslaw Jagiello and his brother Witold, in 1409, shortly before the great battle of Grunwald in 1410. The hunts decimated the rich fauna of the forest. For example when king August III hunted on September 27, 1752, a total of 42 aurochs and 13 elks were killed, not to mention lesser game. The auroch is the European bison, the largest wild animal in Europe, which survived only in the Bialowieza forest. It was threatened with extinction, but in 1921 the Polish government declared the Bialowieza forest a national park and the aurochs were protected. However World War II very nearly finished off the breed. Only 15 aurochs were left. Thanks to intensive conservation efforts they proliferated and now about 300 roam the forest freely. About 30 populate the reservation.

The auroch, a huge animal, is the king of the forest, which is the home of 62 other varieties of mammals, among them the tarpan (a wild horse) the boar, deer of several kinds, the beaver, the badger, and many others. There are also 226 varieties of birds, 20 of reptiles, and 24 of fish.

All these animals were not brought to Bialowieza as to a vast zoo or reservation but have lived there since time immemorial. It is the only large stretch of European forest preserved intact—at least in part—together with its fauna.

Bialowieza should be seen, quite apart from the interest attached to the aurochs and other fauna. Many Europeans, and some Americans too, have forgotten by now what a forest looks like, not a thicket or an impassable jungle, but an honest-to-goodness forest of pine and oak and ash, such as were the woods of many European countries before the 19th century.

It looks big and awesome, dark and mysterious. There is a strange feeling of some powerful presence as one looks round from the crown of a hill to see trees, big old trees, for as many miles as the eye can reach. And there are more trees beyond the horizon. The part kept as a special reservation looks very wild and primitive, for no trees have been cut down there for centuries. As they reach the limit of their age, they fall, perhaps brought down by a gale, and lie rotting untouched by human hands.

Trees many centuries old, of tremendous size, a rich undergrowth of bushes and shrubs, mosses and creepers, berry plants and mushrooms—all create a picture of abundant vegetation, yet different from the tropical rain forest—more austere but less treacherous—a place where there might be goblins and gnomes, benevolent ones.

There are 26 varieties of trees in the Bialowieza forest—mostly oak and hornbeam, maple and linden, fir and pine. In the wetlands there are ash and alder and 55 varieties of bushes.

Some of the trees are 150 feet high with a circumference of 24 feet. It is quite easy to get lost in the forest and it can only be visited with a guide. Any travel office in Poland will help you get there. In this exceptional instance, an organized tour is preferred.

Wieliczka: The Oldest Mine, the Best Asthma Cure

*A*lthough this guide deals mainly with places where one can actively do something rather than passively sightsee, an exception must be made, for the salt mines of Wieliczka—arguably one of the wonders of the world.

Located about five miles from Cracow, the salt mines of Wieliczka were founded by Queen Kinga about A.D. 1290 and have continuously operated ever since. They still produce about 22,000 tons of salt annually.

During the seven centuries of steady operation, hundreds of miles of tunnels and hundreds of shafts were cut out of the solid rock of salt, creating an eerie subterranean world, a giant labyrinth in which one could get lost forever.

The salty atmosphere preserves wood and other substances, so that all the documents recording the enterprise's operation since the 13th century have been preserved in excellent condition, as has the mining equipment used through the centuries. Wieliczka is heaven for a student of medieval technology, for the machines of other eras were largely preserved, if only because it was too difficult to get them to the surface. Unlike buildings and industrial plants above ground, the Wieliczka mines were practically untouched by the many wars which rolled overhead. Actually, the Polish resistance fighters during World War II were well served by the vast maze of secret passages, a perfect hiding place.

The mines are easily reached from nearby Cracow by bus or even by taxi. The entrance is unobtrusive, with a modest window where admission tickets are sold for about half a dollar. In some countries an attraction as unique would be announced by billboards fifty miles ahead, with lavish reception halls, hundreds of stands and shops with every imaginable kind of souvenir, food or beverage, each announced by its own neon sign. Poland is rather backward in advertising and public relations, which may be a blessing, even if it makes some memorable sites harder to find.

As soon as some thirty visitors are there, they are invited inside and greeted by a guide, who warns them about the danger of smoking (there may be flammable gas in the mine) and low doorways, hazardous for tall people.

Then the guide leads his flock into the caverns of mystery. The way is down, on hundreds of steps of a wooden spiral stairway almost as old as the mine itself. At a depth of several hundred feet a narrow tunnel, hewn in salt rock, leads to a vast chamber about the size of an average church, with numerous sculptures in salt, commemorating various events of Polish history. Rock salt can be carved like marble and seems almost as durable.

The narrow corridor continues and leads to another huge chamber, actually a chapel, with amazingly lifelike sculptures in salt, representing the Last Supper, the Lord's Passion, and other religious themes. There are scores of such chambers, astounding by their size and the variety of art work, all of it in salt, except for some wooden sculptures from the 15th century. Owing to the preservative characteristics of salt, the wood is still in perfect condition, without rot or worms.

There are some underground lakes, with water at 30% salt, which is far more than the Dead Sea. Have no fear of falling into one of them, for it would be impossible to drown and the human body would float like a cork on pure water.

The tour of the underground—which includes only a tiny fraction of the entire system—takes nearly three hours, at the end of which the visitors are at a depth of about 1,000 feet, from which they are brought to the surface by an elevator. Though not seven centuries old, it bears little resemblance to the Otis elevators in American skyscrapers. Passengers, packed tight in a small, half-open iron box with no embellishments, are whisked to the surface in a couple of minutes.

Even in summer, the temperature in the mine is about 45° Fahrenheit and the air is very pure, as pollution does not seem to penetrate there. The air is also heavily laced with salt. The salt of Wieliczka is known to be rich in trace elements, crucial in enhancing the function of the immune system, essential in maintaining good health. That is why some physicians advocate—not always successfully—using Wieliczka salt in its original form, without the refining process which eliminates most of the trace elements.

It has been found that asthma and other respiratory ailments can be treated very effectively simply by breathing the air of the Wieliczka mines. A medical institute adjoining the administrative offices of the mine conducts a program under which patients spend several weeks in Wieliczka, much of the time underground, in dormitories arranged for that purpose. I have talked to people who took that cure and they were enthusiastic about its results. All symptoms of asthma disappearing for at least a year. True to their unintentional policy of avoiding publicity, the local authorities keep such cures a well guarded secret. It is true that there are only accommodations for a limited number of patients, but there would be room underground for thousands. The total length of the tunnels and passages is estimated at well over a hundred miles. The tourist route described here constitutes perhaps less than 1% of the entire system built in seven centuries of incessant burrowing.

Had Wieliczka been in another country, by now it would be commercialized and invaded by hordes of sightseeing tourists and patients seeking an amazingly effective treatment. It would then lose most of the charm and authenticity that make it such a unique spot in the world. The time to see it is before that happens.

Czestochowa: The Jasna Gora Shrine

Czestochowa is an industrial city, population 250,000, in southwestern Poland. Although it received its royal charter in 1370, Czestochowa itself would not attract many visitors, but the nearby Abbey of the Pauline Brothers, Jasna Gora, does attract millions of pilgrims and tourists.

It is Poland's principal shrine, home of the famous Black Madonna. Contrary to the guesses of some foreigners, the Black Madonna is not of African origin. She is a 14th century icon, probably brought from Byzantium. Her dark complexion results from many centuries without cleaning or restoration.

Jasna Gora is to Poland and eastern Europe what Lourdes is to France and western Europe. Both are reputed to work miracles: the altar of the Madonna of Jasna Gora is covered with votive offerings from people who insist that their prayers were answered. Be that as it may, hundreds of thousands of people come to Jasna Gora to pay homage to the Holy Virgin and ask her for favors, miraculous or not.

The special role of Jasna Gora in Poland's history was defined by the siege of the abbey by the Swedish army in 1655, when Abbot Kordecki organized the defense and repulsed the enemy while the rest of the country was temporarily overrun by the Swedes. It was, perhaps, since that time that Polish priests learned to defend the faith with arms when necessary. The Black Madonna was credited with defeating the invaders and the scar on her face, left by an enemy soldier's sword, attests to her valor.

Another near-miraculous event occurred in 1945, when the Nazi occupation army was retreating under Soviet pressure. Before leaving, the German commander ordered scores of delayed-action bombs placed under the church and the altar at which the holy picture is displayed. His idea was that the church and the Madonna would be blown to smithereens, killing the monks and as many Russian soldiers as happened to be there. An additional twist was that, since the explosion would occur several days after the departure of the Germans, the Russians would be blamed for it.

The Pauline Fathers discovered the plan and informed the Soviet commander, who ordered his bomb disposal squads to remove the high-explosive charges. No less than thirty-six powerful bombs were found, more than enough to destroy the abbey totally. There was little doubt in the minds of the faithful that the Black Madonna had a hand in the happy ending.

Her renown has grown ever since, and on the major Catholic feast days up to half a million people can be seen from the 320-foot belfry of St. Mary's church.

The abbey of Jasna Gora was founded in 1382 by Wladyslaw of Opole, a prince of the house of Piast. The basilica, originally Gothic, was rebuilt in the 17th century in Baroque style. The defense walls and ramparts, making the abbey a fortress, were built around 1620—just in time to serve well against the Swedish invasion of 1655.

Through many wars, the Pauline Fathers developed remarkable skills in hiding treasure in secret underground caves. That is why Jasna Gora still has a magnificent collection of art works, mostly of religious character, such as centuries-old vestments braided with gold and jewels, chalices of rare beauty, paintings and sculptures, tapestries and sacral vessels.

On the several occasions when John Paul II visited his native Poland, Jasna Gora became the scene of religious rites attended by almost a million people converging from all over the country, perhaps the largest human assembly to be seen anywhere.

The Black Madonna and her home are not only religious, but also national, symbols for the Poles and the pilgrimage to Jasna Gora—sometimes on foot though other transportation is available—is as much an expression of patriotism as of Christian faith.

To see the throng of hundreds of thousands kneeling on the bare ground and joining in a single voice in centuries-old hymns is to understand what Poland is all about. That is why a visit to Jasna Gora should be included in the itinerary of anyone wishing to become acquainted with the nation's spirit as well as its sights.

Cracow

*P*rovidentially saved from destruction in World War II, Cracow is unique: a medieval city preserved almost in its entirety and not as a museum monument, but as a living vibrant community. Shopping in the center of Cracow, one might not notice that the shoe store is in a house five centuries old, its stone threshold worn down by many generations.

Now with a population of 700,000, Cracow's inner city—far from becoming a slum, as is sometimes the case—remains a jewel of architecture, just as it was when Cracow was Poland's capital from the 11th century to the end of the 16th. The bulk of the current population lives in modern suburban developments, while the heart of the city, once circled by defending walls (some of them still stand) has changed little through the ages.

Market Square, at ten acres the largest in Europe, is still the same, with the vast Clothiers' Hall in its center. Originally Gothic, it was restored after a fire in 1555 by Italian architects in Polish Renaissance style. Built as a kind of medieval mall, it still serves commerce from many stalls inside the majestic building. In a corner of Market Square, St. Mary's church reaches to heaven with its two spires of unequal height. In 1241, a watchman at the top of the 280-foot belfry spotted the Tartars approaching. The call of his trumpet was cut short by a Tartar's arrow. To this day, every hour on the hour, from the tall, church belfry a trumpeter sounds a plaintive call, broken in midphrase at the same point—according to tradition—at which the tune was interrupted almost 800 years ago.

The smaller church of St. Andrew, close by, dates from the year 1086, nine centuries ago.

These relics of the distant past convey an idea of the antiquity of Cracow, which has hundreds of other ancient monuments, most of them well preserved or restored to their original state.

There are many illustrated guidebooks of Cracow and qualified English-speaking guides. In addition to the official guides supplied by travel offices or city agencies, there are also many young people who would be happy to show you the city they love. Some of them could be found in the Students' Club in Market Square. They give a more personal touch to the city tour than do the professionals, who usually speak to a group of tourists and deliver the same prerecorded (in their minds) story, sometimes loaded with more detail than one can absorb.

The easiest way of finding individual, personal guides is to look for the nearest college or university and find the English department. The instructors will be glad to give their students a chance to practice their English and the young people welcome the opportunity to talk with a native English speaker and the prospect of earning a few zlotys or dollars.

Cracow has eleven academic institutions, starting with the venerable Jagiellonian University, founded in the 14th century, one of the oldest in Europe. It counts among its alumni Nicholas Copernicus, the great astronomer who opened a new era for science when he declared in 1543 that the sun, not the earth, was the center of our planetary system.

The university buildings dating from Copernican times are among the historic monuments worth seeing.

Other academic institutions in Cracow include such specialized schools as the Academy of Agriculture or the Academy of Mining. All have English courses in their curricula.

The highlight of a tour of Cracow is the Wawel Castle, on a bluff overlooking the Vistula. It was the seat of the kings of Poland from the 11th to the late 16th century, when the capital was transferred to Warsaw. The oldest part of the Wawel compound dates from the 10th century, 1,000 years ago.

A really thorough tour of the royal complex of Wawel could take days, if not weeks. It offers a tangible demonstration of the evolution of architectural styles, as each century brought something new, while the old was mostly conserved. The earliest chapel, dated 10th century, was Romanesque, followed by several stages of Gothic and then Renaissance, which remains the dominant note, as little was changed after the end of the 16th century, when the capital was moved to Warsaw.

The great bell of the Wawel cathedral, called Zygmunt after the king on whose order it was cast in 1520, is one of the largest in the world, with a circumference of 25 feet.

The royal crypt under the Tower of Silver Bells of the Wawel cathedral was the burial place of Poland's kings and later of great poets and statesmen. Marshal Joseph Pilsudski, who won back Poland's independence in 1918, is buried there.

The Wawel castle has been restored to its original condition, which includes the furniture and magnificent tapestries, notably those ordered in Flanders in the 16th century by king Zygmunt August, the last of the Jagiellonian dynasty and the last to reside at Wawel.

Aside from the numerous art works in Wawel castle, there are great artworks in Cracow's several museums. One of them, the Czartoryski Museum, founded by the princes of that name, has such masterpieces as Rembrandt's *Landscape before a Storm* and Leonardo da Vinci's *Lady with an Ermine.* The museum is located in the former Arsenal close to the old city walls. Most of the walls were pulled down in the 19th century and replaced with a garden, but some sections remain, notably one with St. Florian's Gate and the Barbican, which was built around 1498.

In the immediate vicinity of Cracow are several points of interest well worth seeing. We have already dealt elsewhere with the Wieliczka salt mines and Ojcow national park. There is also the Benedictine Abbey of Tyniec, on a high bank of the Vistula. Rather like Wawel castle, the abbey was founded in the 13th century and has served the order of St. Benedict ever since. It resembles a castle, with its six-foot-deep walls and ramparts built to protect it from Tartars or other invaders. The Abbey of Tyniec is not a museum, though it easily could be one. It is still inhabited by monks, though some parts can be visited. Incidentally, there are more clergy, friars, and nuns in Poland today than before the war, even though the current government is officially atheist. Religious tolerance is a very old Polish tradition respected today as it was when Europe was ravaged by wars between Catholics and Protestants, while in Poland these denominations lived side by side in peace.

Another fascinating religious site in the vicinity of Cracow is the shrine of Kalwarja Zebrzydowska (which means the Calvary, that is, the Stations of the Cross) founded by the Zebrzydowski family. A vast complex of 42 chapels and shrines, it represents the Stations of the Cross and is a majestic church and a monastery of the Bernardine Brothers as well. Thousands of pilgrims converge at Kalwarja in the summer and, in procession, follow the path of Jesus in a religious pageant reminiscent of those of Spain.

The buildings are relatively new by Cracow standards. The Kalwarja was consecrated in 1603. It is still beautifully maintained by the Bernardine friars, who also conduct in the abbey a seminary for training priests. Contrary to some other countries, Poland has no shortage of young men who choose to be ordained in the Catholic church.

Kalwarja Zebrzydowska and the Tyniec Abbey can be reached easily from Cracow by bus or even by taxi, which would not be unduly costly.

Warsaw

Warsaw was founded at the turn of the 13th and 14th centuries, but at that time, Warsaw was the capital only of the duchy of Masovia. When the dynasty of the princes of Masovia became extinct in 1526, the province was incorporated to the crown of Poland, which had its capital in Cracow. By the end of the 16th century, however, the royal residence, which was the capital at the time, was moved to Warsaw.

That is why Warsaw is architecturally younger than Cracow and most of its buildings date from the 17th and 18th centuries. Warsaw was less fortunate than Cracow, which escaped destruction through its ten centuries of existence. Located on the main path between western and eastern Europe, Warsaw endured numerous invasions, yet always managed to rise from the ashes. That incredible vitality and will to survive are the dominant characteristics of Warsaw and its people, hardened by blows that would have crushed the spirit of those with lesser mettle.

Cracow saw its greatest days long ago, but Warsaw's finest hour was quite recent, well within the memory of many of its current inhabitants. The horrors of the Nazi occupation during World War II and the great uprising of 1944 are still fresh in the minds of the people of Warsaw: in fact it is the dominant note in the city's collective mind.

To understand Warsaw pride we have to recall the events of the war and the test by fire which the Varsovians passed with honor. Songs have been written about London pride, but the current writer, having spent every day of the "blitz" in London and having witnessed every raid by the Luftwaffe, can attest that it was child's play compared with what Warsaw went through.

At the outbreak of the war in 1939, Warsaw had 1.3 million inhabitants. Surrounded by the German army on September 8, Warsaw resisted until September 27 the two weeks of constant bombardment by heavy artillery and by air. The mayor of Warsaw, Stefan Starzynski, rallied the people to dig trenches and help the Polish soldiers defend the capital. The overwhelming superiority of the Germans in numbers and armaments made the outcome a foregone conclusion, but the defenders made them pay a heavy price in casualties.

Immediately after entering Warsaw, Germans started mass arrests and summary executions of people rounded up at random in the streets. Today, in many parts of Warsaw, you will see commemorative tablets reading: "On the day of . . . 23 persons, lined against this wall, were shot by the Germans." The bullet holes are still there, a memento.

Thousands of people were deported to concentration camps from which few returned alive. The Jews, who constituted about 30% of Warsaw's population, were confined in a section of the city which became known as the ghetto. The victims of the street executions were mostly gentiles, since the Jews were locked up in the ghetto. The Germans soon started sending the Jews to the extermination camp of Treblinka. In the meantime, the Poles formed an underground armed resistance organization, known by its initials A.K., which in Polish stand for Home Army.

161

Following that example, the Jews in the ghetto formed their own resistance, but because of the obvious limitations imposed by the sealed ghetto walls, it was small and poorly armed, though the A.K. smuggled some weapons to the ghetto for the Jewish resistance. On April 19, 1943, an uprising occurred in the ghetto when a group of several hundred young men decided to die fighting rather than in a gas chamber. Their heroic endeavor could not hope to overcome the German army and the ghetto was soon leveled by Nazi bombers and tanks and the remnant of its populace exterminated.

Outside, the arrests and mass executions continued at an accelerated pace, while the German army suffered defeats on the eastern front.

The Soviet army was already very close to Warsaw and the A.K. decided to play an active role by attacking the Germans and setting the city free. On August 1, 1944, a major uprising broke out and about 150,000 Polish resistance fighters seized a large part of the city, while the Germans kept the rest. Front lines formed and heavy fighting continued until October 2, which means that the Polish partisans held the Wehrmacht at bay for more than two months. In the course of the battle 200,000 citizens of Warsaw lost their lives, but the Germans also suffered heavy losses. After the surrender of the surviving remnant of the A.K., the Germans proceeded systematically to destroy what was left of Warsaw, by dynamiting buildings. The surviving population was driven out.

This summary account of the events of the war is important because as one walks Warsaw's streets, one can imagine the city that was killed—literally buried under the rubble—with most of its population exterminated. Yet the city rose from the ruins, restored its institutions, and took great care to bring back the old in the minutest detail. A new Warsaw was created around the old.

It is also important to make clear that there were two

distinct Warsaw uprisings occurring more than a year apart. There was one in the ghetto in 1943, by a gallant group of several hundred brave men. It lasted about two weeks and was confined to a fraction of the city. The other, in 1944, by about 150,000 Polish resistance fighters lasted two months and embraced the entire city of Warsaw. Both were heroic and merit great honor, but there was a vast difference of scale. Often that fact has been overlooked abroad, where many people are aware only of the ghetto uprising and not of the incomparably larger one of 1944.

When viewing the current Warsaw, now a largely modern city of about 1.7 million, one should never forget that it was once wiped off the face of the earth and then rose again, bigger if not necessarily better than before. It takes a good deal of imagination to visualize a community that can lose almost all of its material assets and about a third of its members, then come back stronger than ever. That tenacity is expressed in the first words of the Polish national anthem, "Poland will never perish."

The Old City of Warsaw, totally destroyed by the Germans, was rebuilt after the war with such care that one could never guess that the beautiful 17th century townhouses, authentic down to the doorknobs and wrought-iron gates, were only a heap of rubble in 1945.

The Royal Castle, too, was totally destroyed and now stands on the high bank of the Vistula river, indistinguishable from the old one, inside and out. Special bricks and roof tiles were made, old-fashioned hardware in 17th-century style manufactured, and elaborate plafonds carved and painted to restore the castle to its royal splendor.

The restoration of old Warsaw was assisted by the extraordinarily accurate paintings and etchings of Bernardo Belotto, also known as Canaletto, who was the house artist of the last king of Poland in the 18th century. Not all of the hundred or so old palaces of Warsaw were restored, but those which were now serve as government offices, museums, or headquarters of various organizations.

The restoration, conducted by art experts, aimed at bringing the building back to its original condition. In many cases, this meant going back to the first design, rather than to the condition of the building in 1939 at the outset of the war.

St. John's cathedral in Warsaw's Old City is a good example. The oldest church in Warsaw, it was built at the turn of the 13th and 14th centuries in pure Gothic style, though it did not become a cathedral until 1797. In the intervening centuries, it was renovated several times, with additions reflecting the fashion of the period. Notably in the 1830s the front was covered in English neo-Gothic style, with pinnacles and turrets reminiscent of some British pseudo-Gothic castles of recent date.

The restoration after the last war brought St. John's cathedral back to its genuine medieval Gothic style of austere, clean-cut lines and raw, red brick—imposing in its stern beauty.

The tombstones of the past inside the church remained intact, among them those of Stanislaw and Janusz, the last princes of Masovia, who died in 1524 and 1526, respectively.

Detailed descriptions of other historic monuments in the Old City and elsewhere are to be found in many guidebooks and tourist information brochures easily obtained in Warsaw bookstores and travel offices.

Next to the Old City is the New Town, so called because it was built about a century later, that is in the 15th century. It has many beautiful churches, including St. Mary's (1411), which has a late Gothic-style belfry added in 1581.

Between the old and new cities are the remains of the fortifications that had encircled Old City—a moat, defense walls, and a 16th-century Barbican gate.

Most of the Warsaw palaces outside the Old City date from the 17th and 18th centuries.

The Lazienki Park, designed near the end of the 18th century and combining the natural English landscape and the French formal landscape styles, contains several architectural masterpieces.

The Palace on the Island, built for king Stanislas August, around 1790, is a perfect example of neoclassic style, with some Baroque touches in the interior. It was severely damaged during the war but was later fully restored to its former glory.

Close to it is the open-air theater built in 1790 by the famous architect Johann Christian Kamsetzer. Its amphitheater can hold 1,500 spectators and the stage is on a small island separated from the audience by a narrow strip of water. The permanent backdrop includes columns much like those of the Temple of Jupiter at Baalbek, trees, and statues of classical and modern dramatists. Performances are held in the island theater in the summer.

Bordering on the Lazienki Park, which contains several other historic buildings, is the Belvedere Palace. It was originally built in 1662 for Christopher Pac, chancellor of Lithuania, and owes its name to the scenic panorama of the Vistula seen from its windows. The Belvedere was the residence of Marshal Joseph Pilsudski, Poland's national hero in the period between World War I and II. It is now occupied by the chairman of the Council of State, whose office is equivalent to that of a ceremonial president.

About eight miles south, now on the outskirts of the city, is the royal palace of Wilanow, closely associated with king Jan Sobieski, the victor in the relief of Vienna from the Turks in 1683.

The palace, mainly Baroque, is set in an Italian-style park, which comprises several other buildings of the same period, among them a Chinese summer house and a former riding school, now converted to a museum of Polish poster art.

The main palace houses a large collection of Polish portraits from the 16th century to modern times. They are, of course, mainly portraits of the nobility (in the earlier period) and are an interesting study of physiognomy as well as art.

The few examples of historic monuments mentioned here are only a fraction of what Warsaw has to offer. Many other guidebooks detail the descriptions of such past treasures.

Modern Warsaw—the countless buildings added since 1945—is surely impressive in terms of construction alone, but not necessarily in its esthetic quality. The rows of uniform high-rise apartment buildings in the suburbs are no different from those in any other country. The most striking of the postwar structures, the Palace of Culture in the center of Warsaw, was a gift from Stalin in the 1950s. He was not a man whose gifts one could refuse, whatever their worth. About 700 feet high, the gingerbread building serves at least as a landmark helping the visitor to locate the hub of the city.

Warsaw's charm is in its abundant greenery, the shady residential streets bordered by old trees; the cozy little nooks, lanes, and squares; and most of all, in its people.

Gdansk and the
Tri-City

Gdansk, formerly known by its German name, Danzig, is a major port and city of about half a million, located at the mouth of the Vistula River, Poland's main waterway. Throughout its thousand-year history Gdansk has been the gateway of Poland to the seas and oceans of the world.

The first recorded reference to Gdansk was in A.D. 999, when it was the seat of the princes of Pomerania. Later, under the control of the Teutonic Order of the Knights of the Cross (from 1308 to 1454), it was taken over by the Polish crown and remained under it until the end of the 18th century when it was annexed again by Prussia—that is, Germany. Between 1918 and 1939 Gdansk was a free city under the patronage of the League of Nations and was finally returned to Poland in 1945.

Through most of its history Gdansk had a mixed German and Polish population, but now it is 100% Polish. Some of the most prominent citizens of Gdansk in the past, however, were

POLAND

German, among them Fahrenheit (1666–1735), the physicist to whom we owe the thermometer; the philosopher Schopenhauer (1788–1860) and the modern writer Gunter Grass.

The ancient Hanseatic city (Hansa, in the Middle Ages and since, was an association of Germanic cities for commerce and industry) had preserved many splendid relics of the past, despite the damage wrought by World War II. Perhaps the most impressive among them is the magnificent St. Mary's, a huge Gothic structure. It is the largest church in Poland and can hold 25,000 people.

There is also Arthur's Hall, a late-Gothic mansion built in 1616. Formerly it housed the city guilds and currently it serves as a museum of contemporary art. In Gdansk are several other art museums, which are particularly strong in Dutch and Flemish masters, as Gdansk has always maintained close ties with these maritime nations.

The old city of Gdansk managed to retain or restore most of its ancient buildings and its central section looks today much as it did several centuries ago. As in Cracow, most of the population now lives in modern developments on the outskirts, leaving the historic center largely untouched.

The first shots of World War II were fired in Gdansk on September 1, 1939, by the heavy naval guns of the German battleship, *Schleswig-Holstein*, aimed at the small Polish miltiary outpost of Westerplatte, manned by only 180 soldiers under the command of Major Sucharski. Despite the overwhelming superiority of the enemy and the utterly hopeless situation, the Polish garrison continued resisting until September 7, when the surviving men ran out of ammunition. Today the moument to the heroes of Westerplatte commemorates the first Polish soldiers to give their lives in World War II.

The vast Lenin Shipyard also became a historic spot, for it was there that the Solidarnosc movement was born in 1980.

An electric commuter service, on which trains run every

few minutes, connects Gdansk to Sopot, a seaside resort with a
pier almost half a mile long, and to Gdynia, a major port and a
city of 250,000. Unlike Gdansk, Gdynia has no buildings
antedating the 1920s. It is an entirely modern city, built as
Poland's only seaport during the time when Poland did not
fully control Gdansk (1918–1939).

Gdansk, Sopot, and Gdynia constitute the so-called Tri-
City, as they merge into one continuous urban area, much like
the east coast of Florida between Miami and Palm Beach.
Along the line between Gdansk and Gdynia there is the
ancient Abbey of Oliwa, founded in the Middle Ages and
noted for its magnificent pipe organ. Organ music festivals
held in Oliwa are attended by international artists, in the
Gothic setting of the Cistertian monastery founded in A.D.
1186 by Sambor, prince of Pomerania.

A few miles west of Gdynia along the Baltic coast is the old,
small port of Puck (pronounced Putzk). Now used only by
fishermen, it was the Polish Royal Navy base since 1567,
fortified in 1635. It is a charming old seafaring town, reminiscent of the fishing harbors along the coast of Maine, but much
older. The bay of Puck, protected by the twenty-mile long
breakwater of the Hel Peninsula, is perfect for smaller sail
boats and all water sports.

Wroclaw

*T*he diocese of Wroclaw was established in the year 1000 by Boleslaw Chrobry of the Piast dynasty, king of Poland. Wroclaw was ruled by princes of the house of Piast from 990 to 1335, when it was acquired by Bohemia, later by the Hapsburgs and the Hohenzollerns of Prussia.

Wroclaw is an interesting example of a city whose nationality has changed several times. Until 1945, it was a German city, Breslau. At the end of World War II it was returned to Poland, as a formerly Polish city. It is true that much time had elapsed since the reigns of the Piast princes, but then some nations base their territorial claims on events that happened 2000 years ago. Now purely Polish, the city was settled mostly by people who had to leave the eastern provinces of Poland which were annexed after the war by the Soviet Union, including the cities of Lwow and Wilno. The German inhabitants of Breslau emigrated to nearby Germany.

Another major city in the same situation is Szczecin (the German, Stettin), now the principal Polish Baltic port. Hundreds of smaller towns and villages also went through a similar transformation. It was a migration involving millions of people.

Aside from the emotional attachment of the citizens of Lwow and Wilno to their native cities, the swap was on the whole favorable to Poland, as the ex-German provinces were highly industrialized, while eastern Poland was the least developed part of that country.

Now a city of over 600,000 people, Wroclaw is the home of such industries as the manufacture of locomotives and rolling stock, electronics, machines, chemicals, and textiles.

Old Wroclaw, however, is of more interest to visitors, as factories are pretty much the same the world over.

The oldest section of Wroclaw is located on ground which was formerly an island on the river Oder, the lower course of which forms the border between Poland and East Germany. The port of Szczecin is at the mouth of the Oder.

The cathedral of St. John the Baptist was built on the site of earlier cathedrals, dating from the years 1000, 1051, and 1149. It is a majestic Gothic structure built of stone and brick in the 13th and 14th centuries, with some Baroque additions from the 16th. It was severely damaged during the war and fully restored by 1951. Next to the cathedral is the smaller church of St. Giles, in late Romanesque style, dating from the 13th century and restored in 1953. The nearby museum of the archdiocese contains splendid examples of medieval art, among them a Romanesque chalice, liturgical vestments from the 13th century, paintings, sculptures, and jewelry.

In the immediate vicinity are several other medieval churches, for example one of the Dominican order (1226–1260) and the former Bernardine Abbey, now converted to a museum of architecture.

The market square is surrounded by Gothic townhouses, many with Baroque facades added in the 17th century.

A detailed description of all the historic monuments is

available from other specialized guidebooks easily obtained in bookstores and travel offices. Suffice it to say, Wroclaw is a medieval enclave, lovingly preserved in its original condition.

Wroclaw has ten academic institutions, including a university, an institute of technology, and several specialized colleges; thirteen museums, six theaters and numerous scholarly and cultural organizations.

Wroclaw merits a visit, if only to prove that Silesia is not all coal mines, smelting furnaces, steel mills, and other industry all of which hold little appeal for the average tourist. In Silesia there are other towns with valuable historic relics, but Wroclaw is the capital of the region and it has the most complete medieval quarter.

Biskupin and Archeology

The small village of Biskupin, about 30 miles south of the city of Bydgoszcz in western Poland, offers one of the most amazing sights in Poland, perhaps in all of Europe. It is a complete small town, with a network of eleven streets within a square surrounded by defense walls and wooden pavements, obviously the work of a town planner rather than random building. What is astounding is the date of the construction, about *550 years before Christ*, that is, 2,500 years ago.

The prehistoric settlement of Biskupin was discovered accidentally in 1933, when a local schoolmaster noticed some wooden poles at the bottom of a lake and wondered how they came to be there.

It turned out to be a fortified small township, with ten houses to each of the eleven streets forming a regular checkerboard pattern. The streets were paved with boards, the whole settlement was surrounded by a defense wall and located in the middle of a lake. A sturdy bridge of oak, 360 feet long,

173

connected the island to the mainland, but was designed so that the connection could be broken in the event of a hostile attack. A tall watchtower helped observers see the approach of an enemy in time, while the entry to the island from the bridge was by a gate with massive double doors.

While splendid civilizations already existed around the Mediterranean two and a half thousand years ago, Biskupin is an interesting example of a civilization in northern Europe at that time. It was thought until now that the inhabitants of that region were "barbarians," but the structures and artifacts found at Biskupin suggest that the settlers were more developed than some extra-European tribes are to this day.

The gradual drop of the water level converted the island to a peninsula and the whole island settlement was covered with silt, which acted as a preservative of the wooden structures. Not only the houses, but their furnishings and utensils remained almost intact through twenty-five centuries.

Biskupin was, of course, an archeologist's dream come true and its discovery threw new light on the prehistory of the region now known as Poland. Scientific tests proved beyond doubt the age of the settlement and its study revealed many fascinating facts from the distant past.

It was established that the people inhabiting the area at the time were not invaders from some other part of the world but indigenous Slavic tribes settled there from time immemorial.

The artifacts found at Biskupin, as well as the well-planned fortified settlement, proved a higher degree of sophistication than was formerly ascribed to the peoples inhabiting northeastern Europe in the first century before Christ.

That discovery stimulated active archeological research throughout Poland and diggings revealed many other prehistoric settlements and artifacts. None was as complete and well preserved as Biskupin.

One of the fascinating facts brought to light by archeologists was the lively trade carried on two and three thousand years ago with ancient Rome. It was mostly trade in amber, which was highly prized by the Romans. The so-called Amber Trail ran from Rome all the way to the Baltic, where amber was found then as it is now. The route of the trail is marked by ancient Roman coins found in excavations. The itinerant merchants from the Mediterranean, who may have been Phoenicians, used Roman money to pay for the amber, much for the same reason for which amber is now purchased for dollars. One does not sell valuables for anything but the best currency on the market. The vendor's next problem was where to keep the money. Because there were no banks, burying it seemed the best way. Actually the descendants of the people of Biskupin, who have seen their share of wars and invasions, have been using the same method quite recently.

Considerable hoards of Roman coins have been found along the Amber Trail, notably in the vicinity of the town of Kalisz in western Poland, which existed in old times as a hamlet.

Another consequence of the Biskupin discovery was the awakening of a keen interest in the nation's remote origins. Many books based on archeological research enjoyed wide popularity. For example the *Slavic Geneaology* by Pawel Jasienica became a bestseller by reaching beyond the boundaries of recorded history.

Information based on archeological research into times when no written language existed has this advantage over chronicles: ancient structures and artifacts cannot lie, whereas some historians regarded themselves as creative writers as much as record keepers.

That is why the fact that the Poles are direct descendants of the autochthonous population of the same territory thousands of years ago can be proved beyond doubt and seems to give them much satisfaction.

The vast plain stretching between the Oder and the Dnieper, wide open to invasions in modern times, was not so in prehistoric times. Remember, the entire area of present day Poland was once a thick forest, with people living mainly in some clearings and along the banks of rivers and lakes—as in Biskupin. That is why the Mongol hordes that invaded Russia could not penetrate deep into Poland.

At any rate, Biskupin is well worth a visit as one of the most interesting examples of northern European civilization before the Christian era.

Aviation

The history of aviation in Poland closely parallels its development in other countries, starting with the Wright brothers, Bleriot in France, and other pioneers.

In 1926 Captain Orlinski flew in a Breguet XIX biplane from Warsaw to Tokyo and back, the first trans-Siberian flight and a remarkable feat for its time.

Poland developed an aircraft industry and in the 1930s the RWD was one of the best light aircraft in the world and a winner in many international competitions. The Polish gull-wing PZL fighters were sold to the air forces of several nations, and the light bomber Los designed and built in Poland, including the engines, was fully equal in performance to other aircraft of its class.

Nevertheless, the Polish Air Force was no match for the Luftwaffe, which also defeated the French and very nearly the British air forces. The Polish pilots fought stubbornly and downed several hundred German aircraft, but they could not hope to win. Those who survived the brief campaign of September 1939 went to France and then to Britain, where they played an important role in the Battle of Britain, flying Spitfires and Hurricanes—the eight gun fighters built mostly during the time gained for Britain by Poland's resistance in 1939. The tradition of generations was an important factor in rebuilding Polish aviation after the war. Despite heavy wartime losses, some of the engineers and pilots survived to carry on the work of their fathers. The PZL aircraft plant was revived and again started producing fixed wing aircraft and helicopters. The training of pilots and management of light aircraft aviation were entrusted to the Polish Aeroclub and more than forty local aeroclubs affiliated with it.

Their addresses are:

Polish Aeroclub—Warsaw, Krakowskie Przedmiescie 55.

Bialystok—Ciolkowskiego 2, 15-602 Bialystok (the figure is the postal code)

Warmia Aeroclub—Sielska 34, 10-802, Olsztyn 9.

Warsaw Aeroclub—Ksiezycowa 3, 01-934, Warszawa.

Masovia Aeroclub—Grodzka 9, 09-400 Plock

Lublin Aeroclub—24-205 Radawiec kolo Lublina

Eaglets Aeroclub—the airport, 08-521 Debhin.

Random Aeroclub—Aerobatics Center, 26-600 Piastow, poczta Jedlinsk.

Workers' Aeroclub—Kolejowa 3, 21-040, Swidnik.

Zamosc—Pereca 2, 22-400 Zamosc.

Carpathian Aeroclub—Parachute Training Center—38-400 Krosno

Workers' Aeroclub—39-300 Mielec 1

Rzeszow—36-002 Jasionka kolo Rzeszowa

Stalowa Wola—39-425 Turbia kolo Stalowej Woli

Bielsk-Biala—Cieszynska 321, 43-303 Bielsko-Biala; Zar Gliding School—34-315 Miedzybrodzie Zywieckie

Aviation

Gliwice—airport, 44-108 Gliwice
Rybnik Coal Mining District—44-201 Rybnik, skr. 117 (skr = box)
Silesian Aeroclub—airport, 40-408 Katowice
Czestochowa—ul. N. M. P. 9, 42-200 Czestochowa
Kielce—26-001 Maslow kolo Kielc
Lodz Aeroclub—Aviation Training Center—Lublinek airport, 93-468 Lodz
Piotrkow Aeroclub—Flying Instruction Center; Przemyslowa 48—97-300 Piotrkow Trybunalski
Jelenia Gora—Kreta 27, 58-521 Jezow Sudecki, kolo Jeleniej Gory
Opole—Ozimska 71 d, 45-368 Opole
Wroclaw—Zapolskiej 2/4, 50-032 Wroclaw
Copper Distric Aeroclub—Curie-Sklodowskiej, 59-301 Lubin
Walbrzych—Aleja Wyzwolenia 21, 58-300 Walbrzych
Leszno—Soaring Center of the Polish Aeroclub, 64-100 Strzyzewice kolo Leszna
Ostrow—Kaliska 37, 63-400 Ostrow Wielkopolski
Poznan—Niezlomnych 1, 60-900 Poznan, skr. 1089
Szczecin—Przestrzenna, 1, 70-800 Szczecin-Dabie
Lubusz District—66-015 Przylep kolo Zielonej Gory
Bydgoszcz—Biedaszkowo 30, 85-157 Bydgoszcz
Kujawy Region—Torunska 160, 88-100 Inowroclaw
Pomerania—Bielanska 66, 87-100 Torun.
Wloclawek—87-853 Kruszyn kolo Wloclawka.
Elblag—82-300 Elblag airport
Gdansk—Kilinskiego 53, 80-452 Gdansk-Wrzeszcz
Grudziadz—Center for high performance motorless flight—Lisie Katy kolo Grudziadza, 86-325 poczta Mokre
Slupsk—Kilinskiego 11, 76-200 Slupsk
Cracow—Al. Planu 6-letniego 17, 30-969 Krakow, skr. 17

Podhale Aeroclub—33-314 Lososina Dolna kolo Nowego
Sacza
Tatra Aeroclub—Center for competition parachuting; Lot-
nikow 1, 34-400 Nowy Targ, skr.65

All the provincial aeroclubs have airfields and appropriate
equipment. The standard Polish light plane is the Wilga
trainer, also used for towing sailplanes, agricultural work, and
other duties.

Persons holding pilot's licenses in other countries may rent
aircraft in some of the Polish aeroclubs after passing a flying
test and a medical examination.

Flying instruction is also available at some of the aeroclubs.
Information can be obtained at the Polish Aeroclub headquarters in Warsaw, Krakowskie Przedmiescie 55. Training on fixed
wing or helicopter aircraft can be arranged. The cost of such
training in Poland is considerably less than elsewhere.

Gliding and Soaring

The first gliding flight in Poland was made by Czeslaw Tanski, who flew a simple wing of his own construction in the last years of the 19th century. That is why the annual soaring award of the Polish Aeroclub is called the Tanski Medal.

The first soaring competition was held in 1923 near Nowy Targ in the Carpathian foothills and seven types of Polish designed sailplanes participated. At the second competition, held in Gdynia on the Baltic seacoast, there were twenty-two types of sailplanes, mostly designed and made by their pilots.

In the 1930s the soaring sport gained popularity and in 1929 Grzeszczyk set up a duration record of two hours and eleven minutes, which was soon doubled and then quadrupled. Ustjanowa became a major soaring center, with 2,000 pilots trained there every year. Smaller local centers were formed all over the country, wherever terrain conditions allowed the rubber launching of single-seat training gliders. More than sixty such centers were registered up to 1939.

181

Sailplane design advanced rapidly and Polish sailplanes won international acclaim, notably the Orlik on which Paul McReady broke world records in the United States. A woman pilot, Ms. Modlikowska, set a record of more than twenty-four hours and T. Gora flew a distance of 578 kilometers, winning the Lilienthal Medal. Poland was then among the world leaders in motorless flight.

World War II put a brutal end to Polish gliding—for a time at least. Most of the sailplane pilots served in the air force and many lost their lives in unequal combat against the Luftwaffe. The gliding centers and 1,200 sailplanes were destroyed by the German invaders.

After the war, the surviving airmen began to revive the movement and the first postwar contest was held in Jezow in the fall of 1945. An Institute of Gliding, which became later the Gliding Experimental Station, was founded in 1946 in Bielsko-Biala. The first Polish postwar sailplane, Sep, was built there and flown by Adam Zientek at the international competition in Samedan in Switzerland.

In the years that followed, Polish designers produced many high-performance sailplanes: two seaters such as the Bocian (stork), Czapla (heron), Halny or Puchacz (owl). Also the Mucha (fly) and Foka (seal) series, followed by the Cobra and the famous Jantar in several variations, and many others.

The Jantar Standard 2 has a speed range of 52 to 310 kilometers per hour and is internationally known as a world-class performance motorless aircraft.

There is also the Ogar, a motorized sailplane with a small engine enabling it to take off without being towed, as do most of the gliders and sailplanes.

The Soaring Center of Leszno, in western Poland, is one of the leading institutions of its kind in the world. It was founded on May 1, 1952, an anniversary that has been observed ever since. The Center trains new pilots and offers competition-class pilots the facilities for training. It is often visited by motorless flight pilots from many other countries.

The Center's airfield and its facilities comprise about 200 acres, with numerous buildings, among them a hostel with eighty rooms and a restaurant.

The governing body of the Center, as of all other flying clubs in Poland is the Polish Aeroclub, which continues the traditions of the earlier aeroclubs, the first of which was started in 1898. In the years immediately preceding World War I the Aviata company of Warsaw manufactured aircraft and trained pilots. The Polish Aeroclub, formed after World War I, joined in 1920 the International Aeronautical Federation with head-quarters in Paris.

In the period between the wars several clubs were active, including some run by students. The current aeroclub, which actually has a much broader jurisdiction than its predecessors, is an autonomous agency sponsored by the state.

The Soaring Center of Leszno is only one of the establish-ments operated by the Aeroclub, with which we will deal later.

Foreign visitors to the center are housed in the hostel at the price of $15 a day for room and full board. That charge is mandatory. Other charges are:

Glider flight, $10/hour
Aero tow of glider, $1.40/minute
Winch launching (if available), $3
Motor glider flight, $30/hour
Retrieval of glider by road (car and trailer), $.40/kilometer
Glider trailer hire (when own car is used for recovery), $2/ hour
Dual instruction (training) in addition to flight charge, $5/ hour

For persons bringing their own gliders or aircraft, the charges are:

In addition to the regular tow charge, for the first launch of
an alien glider of the day, $5
For any subsequent launches on the same day, $2
For the first landing of an alien aeroplane, $5
For any subsequent landing on that day, $2

By way of comparison, a Miami company advertises 20-min-
ute glider flights at $39.95 per person, two persons minimum;
that is $79.90 total.

For keeping an aeroplane or rigged glider in a hangar, $2/24
hours
For keeping a de-rigged glider in a hangar, $1/24 hours
For parking an aeroplane under two tons or a rigged glider,
$1/24 hours
For parking an aeroplane over two tons, $3/24 hours

The cost is far less than in other countries, though the
service offered is superior. Package prices could probably be
arranged for training in pilot-license level. The center is not a
commercial, profit-oriented enterprise. Its personnel are all
Polish Air Force officers with a very high level of professional
expertise, men dedicated to the sport of soaring and capable of
giving the best instruction possible.

The site of the center was selected, of course, because of its
favorable atmospheric conditions and the presence of thermal
updrafts essential for successful soaring.

No words can adequately describe the joy of flying like a
bird, in eerie silence and without the brutal thrust of the jet or
the loud roar of the piston engine with its churning propeller.
There is a sense of safety in flying on the wind, not at the
mercy of an engine which might fail and not sitting on several
hundred gallons of fuel waiting for an opportunity to explode.

The sailplane is not fast, though in the hands of a skillful pilot it can fly at 200 miles per hour. Most of the time, it just strolls casually across the sky, giving one plenty of time to observe the country spreading below. It looks quite different from a glider, which seldom flies in a straight line but twists here and there, feeling its way toward a desirable updraft.

It is the most satisfying of sports, giving the intense pleasure of honing the subtle skills required to stay aloft and even fly in the direction of one's choice, not entirely at the mercy of the winds. It is also the safest of all flying sports because the sailplane, unlike powered aircraft, can land almost anywhere and does so at a very low speed, minimizing the risk. One has to watch the weather, of course, but that's what meteorology and radio are for.

There are few places where soaring can be learned and enjoyed in better conditions and at lower cost than at the Leszno Center. Its address is Centrum Szybowcowe Aeroklubu P.R.L., 64-100 Strzyzewice kolo Leszna; phone, Leszno 20-90; TELEX 045462 cwl pl.

The other training center open to foreign visitors is that of Jelenia Gora, in Silesia, about ninety kilometers southwest of Wroclaw. Its address is Aeroklub Jeleniogorski, ul. Kreta 27, 58-521 Jezow Sudecki, phone Jelenia Gora 230-57.

The Leszno Center specializes in performance flying (cross-country flights available). It is active from April to September.

The Jelenia Gora Center offers thermal soaring (in summer) and altitude wave soaring (mostly in the fall and winter). No cross-country flights are permitted. Flying activity is year-round, subject to weather conditions.

In both centers the time of arrival, period of the visit, and proposed activities should be agreed on in advance with the management. Bearers of pilot's licenses should send a copy of the license to the center before their arrival.

The following documents are required before flying at the center: valid glider pilot license, log book with currently confirmed entries, restricted radiotelephone license, certificate of personal accident insurance endorsed for glider flights in Poland, and for minors, permission of parents or guardians.

After arrival at the center the pilot undergoes a dual check in a two seater and he may solo only with the consent of the center's management.

Special requirements for altitude flights (Jelenia Gora) are that any pilot who intends to practice wave soaring should have completed not less than 150 hours of glider flight and fifty aero-tow launches. He should also be rated for cloud flying (appropriate training is available at Jelenia Gora). The pilot may be permitted to fly at altitudes in excess of 4,000 meters (12,000 feet) provided he has undergone examination in the decompression chamber at the Aeronautical Medical Center in Wroclaw, at his own expense, unless he can present a medical certificate of decompression chamber tests issued by an authorized institution.

The charges are:

Renewal examination at the Wroclaw Medical Center, without assessment of fitness for altitude flying, $30
Renewal examination combined with assessment of fitness for altitude flying, $50
Examination for holders of valid pilot's license, for fitness for altitude flying, $30

Pilots and persons accompanying them reside in the center at a cost of $15 for room and full board with three meals a day. Polish high-performance sailplanes are exported to many countries, but perhaps the best way is to try them out and buy them on the spot.

Hang-Gliders

*H*ang glider flying is practiced in several aeroclubs, as a preliminary to piloting high-performance sailplanes. Two centers have regular training courses in hang gliding: the Zar Gliding School near Bielsko-Biala and the Performance Gliding School in Jezow Sudecki, near Jelenia Gora. Both are in Silesia, the southwestern part of Poland.

The Zar center is located in the Beskidy mountain range, a scenic region with three lakes created by dams on mountain streams. Hang gliders are launched from a mountaintop equipped with a lift capable of hauling up hang gliders in open, not folded, form. There is also a hostel with eighty beds and a restaurant at the top of the mountain. At its foot there is an airfield from which all types of gliders can be launched by towing and all kinds of aircraft and gliders can land. The surrounding country offers excellent skiing, with many ski lifts. On the northern slopes there is usually snow in April, even sometimes in May.

The address for information and reservations is Szkola Szybowcowa Zar, 34-315 Miedzybrodzie Zywieckie Kolo Bielska-Bialej

187

POLAND

The Performance Gliding School in Jezow Sudecki, in the Karkonosze mountain range, near Jelenia Gora, is particularly well equipped for hang glider flying, as the starting point at the top of a mountain permits flying in three different directions, depending on the wind. There are also facilities for hauling the glider up from each of the three slopes. At the starting point there is a hostel with twenty-five beds and a cafeteria. Accommodations and a restaurant are also available at the bottom. Flight instruction is carried on throughout the year, with winter sports in the surrounding mountains an added attraction, while in the summer one can explore the many trails in the scenic Karkonosze mountains.

The address for information and reservations is Aeroklub Jeleniogorski ul.Kreta 27, 58-521 Jezow Sudecki kolo Jeleniej Gory.

Few vacations could be more satisfying than one combining gliding and skiing or mountaineering amidst splendid scenery at a mere fraction of the cost of the same thing in Switzerland. Admittedly the mountains are not as high nor the hotels as elegant, but the people may be warmer in their welcome.

Parachuting

*P*arachuting as a sport became popular in Poland in the 1930s when seventeen jumping towers were built in various places for preliminary training. Jumps from balloons and aeroplanes followed. Parachuting championship contests are held every year, with precision landing increasing steadily, notably since the introduction of the wing parachute, which permits steering the descent with great accuracy. Polish parachutists participate in the international parachute competitions and generally place respectably.

Proficiency in parachuting is recognized by awarding badges: silver, gold, and gold with three diamonds, awarded after passing a series of tests, especially of accuracy in landing on a target.

Most of the local aeroclubs have a parachuting division and accept foreign guests, subject to their experience. Novices can also receive appropriate training.

The charges for foreign visitors, payable in dollars, are:

Jump from an altitude of   800–1,200 meters, $12
                         1,300–1,700 meters, $14

1,800–2,200 meters, $16
2,300–2,700 meters, $20
2,800–3,200 meters, $25

The fees include the use of aircraft and parachute; subtract $1 if your own parachute is used.

Information about parachuting can be obtained from the Polish Aeroclub, Krakowskie Przedmiescie 55, 00-071 Warsaw, as well as from the local aeroclubs, though not all of them practice parachuting.

Helicopters

The use of helicopters—outside of the military—is constantly growing and covers a multitude of applications: medical services, surveying, geography, archeology, supervision of railroads and highways, marine rescue, fire rescue, agriculture, construction, traffic control, and more.

The Polish PZL aircraft company started manufacturing helicopters in 1956 and continues to make several models, both light and heavy duty, such as the turbine engined Mi-2.

In the United States, some helicopters bear Polish names: Sikorski, an outstanding Russian engineer of Polish origin, who made important contributions to helicopter development, and Piasecki, a Polish-American engineer who formed his own company to manufacture rotary aircraft.

Helicopter flying as a sport is becoming popular and competitions concentrate on precision maneuvering rather than speed. In the 4th World Championship of Helicopter Flight, held in 1981 in Piotrkow Trybunalski in Poland, the victors were George D. Chrest and Stephan G. Kee (U.S.A.) on a Bell OH-58. Second and third places were taken by West German pilots, flying a Bell 205 and a French Alouette II, respectively.

POLAND

The Polish team of Arthur Szarawara and Henryk Moryc, on a Polish made Mi-2 took the fourth place. Eight other Polish teams, also on Mi-2s, including one women's team, also placed.

Some of the local aeroclubs have helicopters, and persons holding rotary flight licenses could participate in their activities—subject to approval. The head office of the Polish Aeroclub in Warsaw can supply information on the opportunities for such flights.

Ballooning

*I*n the 1920s and 1930s ballooning as a sport gained great popularity in Poland. The balloons used at that time were hydrogen ones; no helium gas was then available in Poland. The James Gordon-Bennett Cup competition, an international contest held annually, was won in 1933 by the Polish team of Burzynski and Hynek, in 1934 by Hynek and Pomaski, in 1935 by Burzynski and Wysocki, in 1938 by Janusz and Janik and in 1983 by Makne and Cieslak—all Polish pilots.

In 1939, a few months before the outbreak of World War II, Polish pilots who had won the Gordon-Bennett several times challenged the world altitude record, held by Lt. Col. Anderson, U.S. Army Air Corps. The title holder was invited as a consultant and was present at the launch held in a canyon in the Tatra mountains. It was necessary to start filling the balloon in a sheltered site because the balloon was several hundred feet high and very sensitive to wind before launching. It was the largest balloon in the world at the time and was considered capable of surpassing the record of about 90,000 feet.

POLAND

I was there as a radio reporter and saw the giant balloon rise slowly as hydrogen filled the gossamer sheath. The spherical aluminum gondola, hermetically tight and pressurized, was still waiting for the crew. The filling took hours. It was night and one could hardly see the top of the balloon, even though it had not yet reached its full height. Suddenly a blinding flash lit the valley for miles around and a violent gust threw me, still clutching my microphone, to the ground. Thousands of cubic feet of hydrogen burned in a split second, but there was no explosion, as the flimsy fabric of the balloon offered no resistance to the expanding gas. Half conscious, I wondered whether I should tell the radio listeners the bad news right away. The whole project was under military control and perhaps I might be breaking security by broadcasting a failure. So I calmly continued my patter about the weather and anything else that came to mind, waiting for an appropriate moment to interrupt the program without sounding alarmed. I wanted to ask the commanding officer what to do next. Permission to release the news of the disaster was granted, but this was the end of attempts to beat the world altitude record with a hydrogen balloon and, in fact, of hydrogen balloons. Colonel Anderson remained world champion for some time, mainly because he had access to helium, which is not combustible.

The cause of the disaster was never established, though it was rumored that German sharpshooters watching the launch from nearby mountaintops might have been responsible. It happened after Munich and Czechoslovakia had already surrendered to Hitler. The mountains on one side of the valley were in Slovakia.

After the war, in the 1960s, balloon sport was revived in Poland. Hot-air balloons were used. Even though they actually carry an open flame, they are much safer than gas balloons. Hydrogen ones are still used occasionally, with caution. Several centers of balloon training were established in Ka-

194

towice, Bialystock, and Poznan, but the main one is at Leszno, close to the gliding center. Balloon competitions are held annually, but no one tries any more to beat the world altitude record. Foreign visitors can enroll in balloon courses at the Leszno center on terms similar to those for gliding.

Retirement in Poland

Many Americans, mostly of Polish descent, live in Poland in retirement. That option, of course, is open to anyone regardless of background, but a person might feel uncomfortable not knowing the language of the country. Yet the reason for retiring in Poland is not patriotic sentiment alone. Simply, it is the fact that a dollar there can buy several times what it can buy in the United States.

Consequently a Social Security pension of about $500 a month, which can keep one barely alive in America, constitutes wealth in Poland.

A retiree can buy a house or an apartment for about $15,000 or less and live very comfortably on about $300 a month, which is about ten times the average salary of the local residents. Under a special agreement between the American and Polish governments, the pension is changed to zlotys at a rate somewhere between the official one and the free-market one.

However if the pensioner's relatives or friends, or even his trustee abroad wish to send dollar vouchers purchased at an Orbis office outside Poland, they can do so legally. The vouchers can be sold in the free market at the going price—now about 3,000 zlotys to the dollar.

I know personally several such retirees living in Poland and they certainly enjoy a lifestyle they could only dream about elsewhere. All the food items which are rationed, especially meat, can be easily purchased at a free-market price, still very low when expressed in dollars. For example veal cutlets, which cost about $8 a pound in American supermarkets, can be had for less than a quarter of that price.

The expatriate retiree is not concerned about the various shortages which trouble the rest of the population, as American goods can be purchased at the Pewex stores for dollars, at prices lower than in the United States. The main drawback is that being the object of general envy may be embarrassing.

Retirees keep their American or other foreign citizenship and can travel abroad as much as they like. They are not subject to any special supervision nor watched by anyone, as the authorities evidently think—no doubt quite rightly—that they are too old to be up to any mischief.

Nevertheless it is advisable to meet some such retirees and discuss with them in detail the pros and cons of the situation before taking any official steps. Talk to several. People's reactions may vary and one person's opinion is not enough.

Names of retirees probably might be obtained through the American consulate.

Retirees may bring a car with them, but it should be preferably a European model with a diesel engine because parts for American cars are very hard to get and diesel fuel is not rationed whereas gasoline is. Some people whose income would be pretty close to the poverty line in America keep a chauffeur and a housekeeper in Warsaw.

When considering retirement in Poland, it helps to remember that the climate resembles Minneapolis more than Miami. On the other hand there is a rich cultural life, especially in the capital, as well opportunities for social life enhanced by the ability to pick up checks without the slightest pain.

Single retirees run an additional risk when they discover with some surprise that they are highly eligible candidates for matrimony with youngsters less than half their age as partners. Some may welcome the chance; the wiser ones will think twice; most will be flattered by the attention regardless of its motivation.

Various legal formalities are required before obtaining the right to establish permanent residence in Poland while retaining foreign citizenship. One of the conditions is proof of an income sufficient for support, but the amount required is not excessive. In any case, a thorough study of conditions should precede any legal steps. Some older people are so set in their ways that they could not easily adjust to a different culture and political system, even if the culture and language are not wholly foreign to them. Others would find such a change an exhilarating experience and a challenge worth taking up. It's up to you to decide to which group you belong.

Adoptions

Poland has the highest birth rate in Europe (19.5 per 1,000 people annually) and a moderate death rate (9.8 as compared with 8.7 per 1,000 people in the United States). Consequently the population increases at the rate of about 300,000 people a year. It is now 38 million and is likely to exceed the 40 million mark in about seven years.

One of the consequences of this situation is a fairly large supply of children available for adoption. They are orphans or children whose parents—more often young unmarried mothers—are unable to bring them up.

If not adopted, such children are raised in public children's homes, institutions that—even with the best intent in the world—are incapable of providing a family's love and personal care. Therefore, they are willing to offer their wards for adoption, after checking carefully the prospective foster parents' credentials.

There is no objection to the children being adopted by foreigners, though preference is given to persons of Polish descent, who can acquaint the children with the Polish language and culture. However, in view of the large supply, many children are adopted by foreign parents who have no connection to Poland. This is due to the low birthrate in most other European countries, notably in Scandinavia. Danes, Swedes, and Norwegians obviously prefer the blond blue-eyed Polish children, which could be their own. In Poland one meets many tall women and men over six feet in height.

The adoptions of children from the public homes are handled by the Towarzystwo Przyjaciol Dzieci (Society of Children's Friends) in each provincial capital (Wojewodztwo) and the provincial Mothers' Children's and Youth Department, which has a commission for foreign adoptions.

Adoptions can be made through other channels also if a mother willing to give her consent can be found. In that case, district courts deal with the adoption formalities and check the qualifications of the prospective foster parents.

As in so many other situations, the assistance of local friends is the best if not the only way of dealing with adoptions. They can contact the single mothers in the maternity departments of hospitals, some of who may be unable to keep their babies for various reasons. If such a mother is found, the court formalities can be handled within a matter of weeks. The prospective parents may have to obtain the consent of their own authorities, possibly through their consulate in Warsaw.

Polish public opinion about foreign adoptions is divided. Some describe them as a reprehensible trade in human beings; others insist that a loving family in another country is better than a government-operated orphans' home in one's own. There is no doubt that in most cases the foreign foster parents can give the child much better care and education than a teenage mother.

The matter surely will remain controversial, but in the meantime, many Polish babies will continue to be adopted by foreign parents.

Buy a Castle!

*P*oland is a land with hundreds of castles, manors, monasteries, and other historic buildings waiting for an owner. They were seized by the government after the war and some of the most notable ones were restored or are in the process of being brought to their former glory as historic monuments. But the government lacks funds for restoring a great many beautiful relics dating from the 15th, 16th, 17th, 18th centuries, some even from the early 19th century. Since their demolition is out of the question, a new policy permits their sale to persons who undertake to restore the building within a certain time—several years, depending on the particular case. The selling price is low, ranging from $5,000 upward, but not to any great heights. Because labor costs remain low, the restoration would not be nearly as expensive as in the West. It would be assisted by the guidance of experts in the art, people who rebuilt the Old City of Warsaw and its Royal Castle.

The idea is that it is in the national interest that these heirlooms of Poland's history not go to waste. Consequently, persons undertaking their restoration as new owners get tax exemptions and other assistance.

The properties available span a wide range, from magnificent castles with drawbridges to charming small country manors or abbeys. Their condition also ranges from near ruin to a structurally sound building requiring mainly cosmetic treatment.

There are 16th-century manors with walls three feet thick, arched ceilings, and fireplaces in which one could roast an ox. There are also elegant country houses with columned porches, much like some antebellum houses in the American South. These would be late 18th- or early 19th-century dwellings. Such manors are invariably surrounded by a park with old trees, often with a pond or two and remnants of hot houses for flowers—all by now rather like a jungle. Included would be stables and servants' quarters, also some farm buildings—though these may have been assigned to local farmers.

Generally speaking, several acres would go with the house, while the rest of the estate has been converted to a state farm or distributed among the populace. Bear in mind that agriculture still remains about 70% private in Poland and farmers own their land, so that socialism is not as prevalent as in the cities.

It is impossible to generalize because of the variety of the properties offered, but there is no doubt that many are extremely attractive. They find relatively few Polish buyers, because few people in Poland have the 40 or 50 million zlotys required. Those who do are not eager to advertise the fact. Besides, the restoration often requires some items that can be purchased only for hard currency, which would be a problem for the local residents. The major component of any construction or restoration project—labor—is extremely low priced, so that the total cost is moderate. Don't be alarmed by the millions referred to here. One million zlotys is roughly equivalent to $350 at the rate applicable to dollar vouchers (bony).

This means that you can become the lord or lady of a charming, stylish manor, with a few acres of land, at about half the price of a one-bedroom apartment in New York City (not on the Upper East Side, where it would cost a great deal more).

Even if one does not buy, looking at a few dozen old castles or manors for sale could be an interesting experience. The way to go would be to consult a lawyer, who could advise you on the legal aspect of acquiring a historic building for restoration. The names of attorneys specializing in that area can be obtained from the Polish Bar Association, Bracka 20a, 00-028 Warsaw, phone 27-13-45 and 27-11-84.

The fees of Polish attorneys are proportionate to those of American attorneys as are the prices of country houses, but make sure that there is no misunderstanding on that point.

To give you an idea of the kind of property you can buy for a song, I will describe one I saw myself. It was a former hunting lodge of king John Sobieski, built in the 17th century of sturdy ash beams, which survived about 300 years in fairly good condition. The house is not large but has plenty of character. Its current owner, who inherited it from his parents, is a 40-year-old engineer and does not know what to do with it, nor does he have the funds required to renovate. In the meantime, he throws parties with rock music and dancing, attended by his young friends. The house and its surrounding park of seven acres, with trees as old as the house, a brook, and a pond with an island in the middle, is registered as a national historic monument. This means that it cannot be razed or altered without the permission of the Curator of Historic Monuments. It can, however, be renovated in its original style and converted to some approved use, for example, a private club or a residence for prominent visitors among other uses. The property includes, in addition to the historic part, about ten acres of open field, which can be developed for other purposes.

In the park there is an entrance to a tunnel, said to run for several miles to the nearby royal palace of Wilanow. The tunnel, reportedly built by Turkish prisoners taken at the battle of Vienna in 1683, collapsed in parts and has not been explored in about 200 years. This property of nearly twenty acres is only about five miles from the center of Warsaw and less than three from the Warsaw international airport. A multilane expressway passes half a mile from the gate. Yet, as I discovered, few people seem know about it. This is typical of Poland, a country full of surprises.

Seeking Roots

There are about 10 million Americans of Polish descent, some of them third or fourth generation, who have lost contact with their families in Poland. Actually the first Polish settlers in America were those who landed in 1608 in Jamestown in Virginia, twelve years ahead of the Mayflower pilgrims in 1620. Captain John Smith, the leader of the Jamestown colony, had spent some time in Poland and deliberately recruited Poles, whom he considered good material for pioneering in the new world.

Whether any descendants of the Jamestown pioneers are now living is unknown, but they were followed by millions of others, mainly at the turn of the 19th and 20th centuries. Their grandchildren are now 100% American and know little about the country of their ancestors.

Yet some of them might be interested in the land of their forefathers and their kin still living there. In fact, the Polish Genealogical Society, 984 Milwaukee Avenue, Chicago, IL 60622 may be helpful preliminarily—before traveling to Poland.

Tracing family histories in Poland may not be as difficult as one would think. Catholic parishes keep their birth, marriage, and death records indefinitely—for centuries. It is also true that some records were lost in the numerous wars which swept the country, but most of them are still there. If the name of the town or village is known, there is a good chance of finding relatives even after several generations.

The current Polish administration keeps records of the population, because every person moving to a new address must report it to the authorities. It would be possible to trace persons bearing your same surname, providing that it is not Kowalski—the Polish equivalent of Smith or Brown. The best way to trace relatives in Poland would probably be by placing small advertisements in the classified section of several newspapers. The cost would be insignificant, but the results might be positive, as such advertisements are read very carefully by thousands of people. There are not very many such searches, so they attract special attention. If the family is still in existence, it would no doubt be found.

In the period immediately following the last war, major population shifts occurred in Poland. Poles from the eastern provinces annexed by the Soviet Union, notably from the cities of Lwow and Wilno, moved in large numbers to the western provinces recovered from Germany and such cities as Wroclaw or Szczecin. It is there that one would now look for families formerly living in the eastern provinces.

Religion

Poland is a predominantly Catholic nation and the church plays a very important role in its life. Whatever your religious affiliation, it may be interesting to see churches packed to capacity, with a crowd listening to the service outside through loudspeakers. Catholics might also appreciate the opportunity to attend a traditional service in Latin—with Gregorian chant, no longer heard in Catholic churches in most other countries.

Incredible though it may seem, the present Poland, under a government that officially proclaims itself atheist but that tolerates all religions, has twice as many churches, more bishops and clergy than the pre-war Poland which recognized Catholicism as the dominant religion.

The famous shrine of Czestochowa with its Black Madonna (black only because the painting is several centuries old and was never cleaned) is certainly among the sights not to be missed. Even more arresting, perhaps, are the pilgrimages to the holy shrine. Formed by a parish, a school, or some local organization, they proceed to Czestochowa on foot—sometimes a distance of several hundred miles. They do so not because they lack other transportation, as there are plenty of trains and buses going to Czestochowa, but as a form of penance attesting to the intensity of one's faith. To see a joyful band of about a hundred people, young and old, men and women, marching in the hot summer sun as they sing religious songs is to understand what Christian faith means to the Poles. That dedication was redoubled when Karol Wojtyla, archbishop of Cracow, was elected John Paul II, Vicar of Christ and Bishop of Rome.

When he visits his native land, which he has done three times, he is welcomed by crowds of up to a million people in one spot. Unlike the only other crowds of comparable size— the ones attracted by sports events and noted for rowdiness— these gigantic assemblies are always orderly and free of misbehavior, even though they are supervised only by volunteer marshals, without any state police. These memorable events demonstrate in a very practical way the control which the church can exert on the Polish people, all the more remarkable for being free of any coercion or means of enforcement other than moral influence.

Foreign visitors, Catholic or not, can always expect a warm welcome in a Polish church. Traditionally the pastor of a parish is ready to extend help and advice not only to his flock, but also to strangers. Especially in rural areas, the parson is often the best source of information on any subject, not necessarily connected with religion.

The office of the primate of Poland, Jozef Cardinal Glemp, is located in Warsaw, at Miodowa 17/19, phone 31-52-31.

Although about 95% of the Poles are Catholics, other denominations are also represented. Their members might be interested in meeting Polish coreligionists and we accordingly list the addresses of their offices in Warsaw.

Lutheran Church: Miodowa 21, phone 31-51-87
Methodist Church: Mokotowska 12, phone 28-53-28
Mormon Church: Falata 6 m.28

Religion

Orthodox Metropolitan of Poland: Swierczewskiego 52,
  phone 19-08-86
Polish Baptist Church: Walicow 25, phone 24-27-83
Polish National Catholic Church: Wilcza 31, phone
  21-18-42
Religious Union of the Jewish Faith: Twarda 6, phone
  20-43-24
Seventh Day Adventist Church: Foksal 8, phone 27-76-11
United Evangelical Church: Zagorna 10, phone 29-52-61

The Polish Language

The Polish language is probably neither more nor less difficult than any other. The pronunciation, although at first
startling to the English speaker, can be mastered once the
sound values of the principal consonants and vowels are mem-
orized. The spelling is almost entirely phonetic, that is to say
every letter represents only one sound. This makes Polish
actually a much easier language to learn than one in which
you never know how to pronounce a word, even though you
can pronounce each separate syllable. Without going into
learned linguistic theories I might point out a few principles
helpful to the beginner:

All the letters in a word are pronounced. *Never leave any
out when it seems to you there are a few too many.*

A   is always pronounced as in *master,* never as in *cat.*
E   is always short, as in *leg,* never long, as in *legion.*
I   is always short, as in *if,* never long, as in *kite.*

J is always pronounced like *y* at the beginning of a word, as in *yard*.

Ch and *h* are both pronounced exactly alike, as in *horse*.

Cz is pronounced like *ch* in *Charlie*

Sz is pronounced like *sh* in *shop*.

Rz and *ż* are pronounced exactly alike, rather like *j* in *jar*.

W stands for *v* and is always pronounced as in *Victor* (Polish, Wiktor).

Y is always short as in *levy*, never long as in *bye*.

Pronounciation

The Polish sounds expressed by ż, ź, ń, ć, ś, ą, ę and ł are difficult to explain on paper and the best one can do for a start is to ignore the little symbols above or below these letters and try to get the others right, especially the consonants. Later on, the ear will detect the vast difference between a simple c and a ć The pronunciation given in brackets after the words in the list below is not meant to convey anything but the roughest idea of what the word may sound like. It would be impossible to transcribe the pronunciation of Polish words more accurately without having recourse to phonetic symbols, probably less intelligible to most readers than the Polish spelling itself. No pronounciation means that the word is so easy that you would only be offended by the suggestion that you could not pronounce it without assistance.

The phrases are arranged to follow the traveler's trend of thought, from such necessities as flying to luxuries like getting a shave. The Polish version is given first, on the assumption that one has to understand before making oneself understood, but if you wish to reverse the process, do so by all means.

There are some good English–Polish dictionaries and books of current phrases useful to a foreign visitor. They can be obtained in bookstores in Poland and abroad.

A few phrases

Nie umiem po polsku: I don't know Polish (Nye umyem po polsku).

Czy Pan mowi po angielsku?: Do you speak English (Chy paan moovi po angyelskoo)?

Francusku: French (frantzouskoo).

Niemiecku: German (nye-mietz-koo).

Jade do Warszawy: I am going to Warsaw (Yadem do Varshavy).

Jade z Warszawy: I am coming from Warsaw (Yadem z Varshavy).

Kiedy odchodzi pociag do Berlina? When is the train to Berlin due to leave (Kyedy odhod-zi potziong do Berlina)?

Prosze mowić powoli: Please speak slowly (proshe moovitz povoli).

Czy może mi Pan pomóc? Can you help me (chy mozhe mi pan pomootz)?

Bardzo Panu dziekuje: I thank you very much (to a man, Bar-dzo panoo dzenkuye; to a woman, Bardzo Pani dziekuje).

Gdzie jest wyjście? Where is the exit (Gdzye yest wyestze)?

Gdzie jest tualeta? Where is the lavatory (Gdzye yest tooalettah)?

Czy tedy droga do—? Is this the way to—(Chy tendy drogah do—)?

Prosze o szlanke wody? May I have a glass of water please (Proshe o shklankeh vody)?

Która jest godzina? What time is it (ktoorah yest god-zinah)?

Ile sie nalezy? How much do I owe you (Ile sien nalezhy)?

Szukam dobrego hotelu: I am looking for a good hotel (shukam dobre-goh hotelu).

Prosze o pokoj dwuosobowy: I want a double room (proshe o pokooy dvuosobovy).

Czy moge miec kapiel? Can I have a bath (chy mogem mietz kompyel)?

Prosze to naprawic: Please repair this (proshe to napravitz).

Szukam Pana Johnsona: I am looking for Mr. Johnson (Shukam . . .).

Ile kosztuje ten kilim? What is the price of this tapestry (Eele koshtuye ten kilim)?

Prosze pokazac mi inne obrazy: Please show me other pictures (Proshe pokazatz mee inn-e obrazhy).

Jest za goraco: It is too hot (Yest za gorontzo).

Czy Pan—? Do you—(to begin interrogative sentence), *Chy Pan* for men, (*Chy Pani* for women)?

Gdzie trzeba wysiadac? Where does one get off (gdyze tsheba vysiadatz)?

Prosze mnie ogolic: Please give me a shave (Proshe mnye ogolitz).

Dziekuje: Thank you (dzyeŋkuyeh).

Dzien dobry: Good morning.

Dobry wieczor: Good evening (dobry viechoor).

Dowidzenia: Goodbye (dovidzenyah, analogous to au revoir).

Przepraszam: I beg your pardon (psheprasham).

Ile: How much (eeleh)?

Vocabulary

about	o
above	nad
always	zawsze (zavshe)
arrival	przyjazd (psy-yazd)
because	bo (boh)
but	ale (aleh), also albo
changing trains	przesiadanie (pshesyadanyeh)
cheap	tani (tanee)
day	dzien (dzyen)

213

days

Sunday	Niedziela (nyedzyela)
Monday	Poniedzialek (ponyedzyaleck)
Tuesday	Wtorek (vtoreck)
Wednesday	Sroda (srodah)
Thursday	Czwartek (chvarteck)
Friday	Piatek (pionteck)
Saturday	Sobota (sobohtah)
dear	drogi (drogee)
departure	odjazd (odyazd)

even	nawet (navet)
express train (prime)	pospieszny (pospieshny)
for	dla
from (someone)	od

he	on
how	jak (yak)

I	ja (yah)
in	w (v)

Miss	Panna (use only with name)
month	miesiac (myesiontz)

months

January	Styczen (stychen)
February	Luty (looty)
March	Marzec (mazhetz)
April	Kwiecien (kvyetzen)
May	May (maay)
June	Czerwiez (chervyetz)
July	Lipiec (lypyetz)
August	Sierpien (sierpyen)
September	Wizzesien (visheshyen)
October	Pazdziernik (pazdzyernick)
November	Listopad (listopahd)
December	Grudzien (grudzyen)

The Polish Language

Mr.	Pan (pahn)
Mrs.	Pani (use for married and unmarried woman)

never	nigdy (nigdyh)
night	noc (notz)
no	nie (nyeh)
nothing	nic (nitz)

numerals

one	jeden (yeden)
two	dwa (dvah)
three	trzy (tshy)
four	cztery (chtery)
five	piec (pients)
six	szesc (shestz)
seven	sieden (syedem)
eight	osiem (osyem)
nine	dziewiec (dzyevyentz)

ten	dziesiec (dzyesyentz)
first	pierwszy (pyervshy)
second	drugi (droogi)
third	trzeci (tshetzi)
fourth	czwarty (chvarty)
fifth	piaty (pionty)
sixth	szosty (shoosty)
seventh	siodmy (syoodmy)
eighth	osmy (oosmy)
ninth	dziewiaty (dzyevonty)
tenth	dziesiąty (dzyeshonty)
eleventh	iedenasty (yedenasty)

(Note: If the numbers describe hours, the numbers would end in *a*, for example, the eleventh hour would be spoken *yedenasta*.)

once	raz

passenger train	osobowy (osobovy)
perhaps	może (mozhe)

please	prosze (proshe)
porter	tragarz (tragash)
she	ona
thou	ty (familiar form of *you*, used with children and close friends)
today	dzis
to (somewhere or something)	do
tomorrow	jutro (youtro)
train	pociag (potziong)
under	pod
vacant, free	wolny (volny)
very	bardzo (bardzoh)
waiting room	poczekalnia (pochekalnyah)
week	tydzien (tydzyen)
what	co (tzo)
when	kiedy (kyedy)
where	gdzie (gdzyeh)
where from	skad (skond)
where to	dokad (dokond)
who	kto
why (what for)	poco (potzo)
why	dlaczego (dlachegoh)
with (or from)	z
without	bez
year	rok
years	lata
lyes	tak (tahk)
yesterday	wczora, (vchoray)
you (group)	wy (vhy)